# Perfect Love

UFUOMAEE

**PERFECT LOVE**

Copyright © 2018 Ufuomaee

All rights reserved.

ISBN: 9781719846004

This is a purely fictional work. Any resemblance to real persons, organizations or events is merely coincidental.
This story is not appropriate for children and the mentally unstable. Parental guidance is advised for children under 16.

Photo credit: www.pixabay.com
Unless otherwise stated, all Scriptures referenced are from www.blueletterbible.org.

All rights reserved. No part of this book may be reproduced, stored in a retrieval system, transmitted in any form or by any means-electronic, mechanical, photocopying, recording, or otherwise-without prior permission in writing from the copyright holder.

# DEDICATION

*"They that are whole need not a physician; but they that are sick. I came not to call the righteous, but sinners to repentance"* (Luke 5:31-32).

# AUTHOR REVIEWS

*** 

"You constantly allow God use you to correct the misinformation and vices in our world today and you do it in such a way that everyone gets the point. You really are amazing!"
- *Ifeoluwapo Alatishe* -

"Ufuomaee is a realist (I love the fact that she includes happenings in the society in her stories, sensitive topics we don't like to talk about. For instance, of sexual abuse in the Church and home as portrayed in The Church Girl and Broken respectively). Ufuomaee has that magical power to keep her readers spellbound. I also love the fact that she writes from a Christian perspective."
- *Jesutomilola Lasehinde* -

"Truly, you are one of the few people I delight in reading their posts. You make the book so real, I sometimes see myself as one of the characters. And I've been blessed by your books. You have a unique style of portraying your characters. You give them life."
- *Folashade Oguntoyinbo* -

"Ufuomaee is an author that writes fiction as though it is real. A Christian not ashamed to put her values into writing and I find myself reading the Bible passages she puts at the beginning of her stories. A great author whom everyone needs to read from."
- *Jimi Kate Darasimi* -

# CONTENTS

|    | Acknowledgments | i      |
|----|-----------------|--------|
| 1  | The Prologue    | 1      |
| 2  | Volume One      | Pg 4   |
| 3  | Volume Two      | Pg 22  |
| 4  | Volume Three    | Pg 41  |
| 5  | Volume Four     | Pg 59  |
| 6  | Volume Five     | Pg 80  |
| 7  | Volume Six      | Pg 102 |
| 8  | Volume Seven    | Pg 120 |
| 9  | Volume Eight    | Pg 138 |
| 10 | The Epilogue    | Pg 169 |
|    | About The Author| Pg 173 |

# ACKNOWLEDGMENTS

I give God all the glory for this story. I had such an interesting experience writing it. I had many moments when the inspiration was flowing, and moments when I wondered at what a mess the story was becoming! How could they ever come through after such betrayal? But God always finds a way and I was pleased to be used to communicate His Perfect Love through this story.

I want to thank my patrons at blog.ufuomaee.org and on Patreon.com for believing in me and encouraging me in this ministry. It means everything. You give me the confidence to keep writing, and of course, the push, so that I can entertain and inspire you with more stories. Thanks so much!

To everyone who buys and read my books, I'm truly grateful. Thanks for spreading the word, dropping your reviews and encouraging your friends and family to get their own copies too.

Special thanks to Wale Oyepeju for sharing his insights about the world of script writing with me, so that I could write a believable story ☺.

Finally, much love to my family, my rock, my home; Toju, Jason, Mom, Dad, Rhe, Kiwi, Jite and Ekechi. Thanks for always being there, inspiring and supporting me in your own special ways.

# Perfect Love

UFUOMAEE

# PART ONE

*"Flee fornication. Every sin that a man doeth is without the body; but he that committeth fornication sinneth against his own body"*
(1 Corinthians 6:18).

# THE PROLOGUE

"*Many waters cannot quench love, neither can the floods drown it: if a man would give all the substance of his house for love, it would utterly be contemned*"
(Songs of Solomon 8:7).

My earliest memory of romantic love was from the movie "Endless Love". That was the definitive romantic story for me. Not even "Romeo and Juliet" came close. It would be many years before I learnt that it was actually considered a "blue film", and not at all appropriate for impressionable children.

However, besides the lust and sex that seemed to define the movie, it was the heated emotions that burned between the lovers, despite the opposition from their families, that stayed with me. I wanted that kind of reckless love; a mad love, ungoverned by reason and driven entirely by passion. Even when I became a Believer, I always held out hope to have such a fiery romance. And not just romance, marriage.

But many years later, real life changed all that and I was about to marry someone for whom my heart didn't burn. I'd given up on love, as I knew it. Because my heart had been broken, and they said love is not about emotion, but an act of the will... But when the one for whom my heart once burned returned into my life, I realised that, truly, "*the heart wants what it wants...*"

Alas, ours was not the "forever love" kind. I was his toy, and he was my everything. And when he was done, so was I. And I didn't dare to dream that I'd ever find the kind of mutual, passionate and enduring love I desired. I took comfort in God, and was happy just to have Jesus, and to be content in Him. Or so I thought.

Mine was a wandering heart. A restless heart. A troubled heart.

It got to a point that I had crushes on almost every single man around me. I just wanted love. Marriage. The perfect romance.

And then I met Temi.

He was not the usual guy that I got hot for, but he was attractive and Christian. We were similar in some ways. We were two idealistic people with dreams, who were committed to or lazily following our passions, depending on how you looked at it.

As a Computer Engineer, he was very bright, and also ambitious. He dreamt of and talked about how he'd be the next Bill Gates by creating some revolutionary software. I liked that he had dreams and a drive. Though he was out of a job at the time. He had potential and lots of confidence.

I was working in a job to fulfil all righteousness. I didn't want to be dependent on my affluent parents to take care of me and chose a job I was sure I would do well in, while I chased my passion of becoming a writer. As a Bank Marketer, I wasn't using my degree in Accounting, a course I'd taken to appease my father, who was the greatest Accountant Lagos had ever known in his time. He now chairs a number of financial institutions, including the one I was marketing for.

So, one day, I met Temi when I was on a marketing run to a Telecomms company. He had just completed an interview for a job there, and we left the building together. As we rode the elevator, I was reading a book on my Kindle device.

"Good book?" he asked.

"Hmmm hmm…" I muttered in response.

"What's it about?"

I sighed and looked up briefly from my reading. He was tall and dark skinned. Not my flavour. So, I gave him a curt response. "Christianity and Evangelism."

"Interesting. It's rare to see beautiful women reading. And about Christianity too," he mused. And I thought it was funny that I was irritated about being disturbed while reading a book about evangelism, instead of seeing that as an opportunity to witness to him. Just as the elevator doors opened, he asked, "Do you mind if I ask what you do?"

It was obvious that he wanted to talk, and well, it was time I actually put to practice what I was learning about seizing opportunities to proclaim Christ. So, after he asked his third question, I decided to put the device away and engage him in conversation.

"I'm a marketer by day and a columnist by night," I said, with a grin.

"Hmmm... A go-getter and an influencer. You sound like someone I'd love to know," he drawled and I giggled despite myself. And when he smiled, I thought he looked like a movie star. And so, when he asked for my number, I didn't hesitate.

Still, I played hard to get, though not for too long. I liked that even though he didn't have much financially, and he knew my background, he was not deterred from coming after me. He showered me with attention, listened to me and read my writings, and believed in my dream to write stories that would change the world. He promised me his love and care. He said he wanted to give me the world and I believed him.

I followed him to Church and it was there that I began to fall for him. I saw him in his element, a passionate follower of Jesus Christ who, though poor, claimed the riches of Christ. And I didn't dare to judge him by his present circumstance. I saw a man of promise, and most of all, a man who saw promise in me.

And even though I never did fall with complete abandon, I said "Yes" to him the day he asked for my hand in marriage, in the presence of our friends and family, after only three months of dating. Because "*love is an act of the will...*" Or so they said.

# VOLUME ONE

*"Casting down imaginations, and every high thing that exalteth itself against the knowledge of God, and bringing into captivity every thought to the obedience of Christ..."*
(2 Corinthians 10:5).

## ONE

Temi and I have been married for over five years now. Ours was a lukewarm kind of love. It was neither hot nor cold and, overtime, it made me emotionally sick. Our little ember flame from the days of our courtship had completely burnt out by the time we celebrated our first anniversary. And by then, we'd already welcomed Lara into our home. And I was miserable.

I'd chosen and laid my bed, and after years of grumbling that it wasn't what I thought it would be, I finally accepted that truly, it was my destiny. I made peace with the misery. It was my constant companion and my muse. It was even the inspiration behind my first book, "Is This Love?".

After years of being turned down by traditional publishers, I finally decided to take the bold step and publish it myself last month. And now finally, in the wake of a New Year, I have the physical copy in my hands. And I'm happy. At least this dream is still alive. But I should have known that I couldn't run from the other forever...

***

It was just an ordinary day when the seams of my fragile world began to unravel. In fact, it was better than ordinary. Just a little bit.

# PERFECT LOVE

You found me on a day I was smiling. I was actually happy, and not looking like the usual mess that has become my image of late. I'd actually bothered to brush my hair that day, before packing it back. Yes, it's due for relaxing, but money's been tight lately, so I'm still putting off doing my hair for a big event...

Anyway, I had just come out from delivering my books to a nearby supermarket, and I was feeling chuffed with myself. I was checking out something on Instagram when I heard someone call my name. I turned around and saw that it was you... And I caught my breath, ever so slightly. I composed myself pretty quickly I think.

Seeing you again was the last thing I needed... But somehow, I knew I'd longed for it. It seemed almost cosmic, like I had called out to you and you'd heard me. Because just a couple of days ago, I found myself looking for you on Facebook or was it Instagram? Of course, I knew I wouldn't find you, because you'd blocked me years ago. Still, I couldn't help but wonder how you were and what you were up to.

Then you showed up, and I knew. You were doing awesome! You looked happy, and healthy and rich... Life has been good to you.

You drove a shiny, black, apparently new and expensive saloon car. I have never really been the materialistic kind, so I didn't stop to look at the make or model. I was just focused on making the most of this meeting with you, knowing I was probably not going to see you in a long, long time.

I remember the last time I saw you was at your best friend's wedding, some years back. I actually forgot when exactly, but you reminded me. My memory's shit these days, and we could agree on that when I congratulated you on a marriage that was almost four years old, thinking it was just last year...

Yeah, so you're married. With kids! Wow. You're really gone. Out of my reach... Not that I am free myself... My awareness that I am also bound in marriage is only one of the reasons we can never be together again.

The real, *real* reason is that you don't love me. That was why we didn't work out... And knowing this is like a bullet to my heart. No matter what happens, even if we succumb to lust, the fact that you don't love me would leave me ruined...worse off than I am now. So, it's really better I don't even think about that!

Looking back at our conversation that day, I can't help but feel so foolish. In some ways, I did better than I thought I would if I ever saw you again. I didn't ignore you. I didn't run away. I didn't get angry and bring up the past hurt. And I didn't ask for your number!

It came up - in my mind - but I immediately dismissed it, because we have been there...done that, and well, I can never live through such pain and humiliation again! I knew if you asked, I'd say "No". I believed I would. It's the only wise thing to do. What good could ever come from having your contact...?

It's bad enough that you told me where you live... I was shocked to realise that we are actually neighbours. Well, I couldn't pin point the block of apartments you said you lived in, so I know I couldn't do anything with that useless information. All it does now is leave me with wonder and anticipation about if I would ever see you again... Maybe you'd come to the supermarket one day, while I am doing some house shopping. Or maybe you'd drive by when I'm returning to my car from an errand or something...

But yeah, I just find myself looking in the direction of your home, whenever I go shopping there, wishing I didn't know where you lived... Wishing I didn't know anything about you. Wishing you'd stay dead and gone...and I would never have to confront the fact that, ten years later, I still want you...

# TWO

I wrote a poem for you. Can you believe it? After everything you put my heart through. After the pain and disgrace, seeing you again, talking to you again still has such an impact on me.

I know I can never go back to being that girl. I am so much more than that. I have learnt so much about myself, about my God and about my purpose. You are not a part of it. You are my enemy.

You are poison to me! Toxic! Just being in your presence again, and I realise how much I want you and how I can never have you, because you would take and leave me empty...feeling worthless yet living for you.

You were my fix, and I now realise that I will probably always be addicted to you. But you're no good for me. Yet, the pull is so strong. I know better now, but I keep wondering if only...

If only you had loved me, would I be married to you today? Would we be happy? Would I have your children and be living a wonderful life? Would you be the spiritual leader I need in a husband?

Or would you take me for granted? Would you fall out of love with me? Would you break my heart? Would you cheat on me? Would you want more than I can give?

And now I do wonder... Are you happy? Is she the one you had always wanted? Is she everything you dreamed she would be? Do you ever wish you'd chosen me? Do you ever think of me?

But all of these don't matter. Not for a minute. Because you are married to her. And she has given you two beautiful children. A girl and a boy. If you don't love her, you are wicked! And truly, why should I desire such?

I should be happy for you. In a way, I am. I am only disappointed that it wasn't us. That together forever was never our destiny, though it was all I once hoped for. But you were not the man for me then. And most certainly are not the man for me now.

I do wonder if I would have felt this way…if I would still desire you, if I was happily married myself. If my husband was all I hoped he would be… If he loved me with all his heart and soul… If we were the best of friends… Maybe I wouldn't envy you. Maybe I would feel bad for you… Or maybe I wouldn't even care or wonder about you…and just be thankful that you let me go so that I could discover real love.

But what's done is done. What is is all there is… I messed up the first time. I can't keep messing up. I can't keep letting you be my Achilles' heel…my weakness.

I have to be strong. For myself. For my family. For my ministry…

Yes, as a Christian, I am a minister of the Gospel of Christ. And there are many people who are looking up to me for a good example. An example that it is possible to do right in the face of temptation. An example that there's life and joy after failure and redemption. An example that faithfulness in marriage is possible, when Christ is involved.

And so I see that that's all you are and will ever be to me. My temptation. But I can defeat you. I will get over seeing you again, and I will focus on my marriage. My ministry. I will do it to the glory of God. So…

"What did you get?" Temi interrupts my thoughts and takes one of the bags I've brought in from shopping to inspect its contents.

"Just a few breakfast things we needed…" I say, as I carry the other two bags to the kitchen.

"Cornflakes? Honey? *Toilet cleaner?* Where's the meat and ingredients for soup?"

"I'll get those at the market later. We were out of eggs and stuff, so…"

"You don't know how to manage money, I swear. You even bought *Kellogg's*! We need food that we can eat, and you're spending all our money on expensive cereals and cleaning supplies!"

"We need to keep a clean house too!"

He hisses and goes back to his armchair, mumbling as usual at my inefficiency. And I sigh and complete my motivational self-talk. *So help me God!*

# THREE

You shouldn't have told me where you live. Now I am constantly looking out for you, wondering if I will bump into you again. As it happens, whenever you discover something new, you tend to notice it a lot more, and see it in almost anything.

Before I saw your car that day, I never knew such a car existed. And then I saw it again. Yesterday, parked by the Church near my home. How weird is that?!

I knew it was the same car, whether or not it's yours, because the look of the car is distinctive. It is beautiful. And I stopped to admire it, and saw that it was indeed a Mercedes Benz, and what I believe is the latest model too. You have good taste...

So, I'm guessing you attend my local Church now... How is it that I never spotted you before? Are you new to my neighbourhood? What evil wind brought you to my doorstep?!

Now, I have to be concerned with looking my best when I leave the house, just in case I bump into you again?! Believe me, I'm not doing it for you, but for me! I don't need you feeling sorry for me or looking down at me in anyway. When you see me, I want you to see that I'm doing fine too, living and enjoying my life without you. And please, don't bother to say hello!

"Hey! Funny to see you here again..."

*What the???* I slowly turn around, my heart in my throat, because I know that it is you, and I'm not ready to see you again. *Are you stalking me?*

"Hey..." I finally say, trying on an average smile. Not too big, so you don't think you made my day and not too small, so you think I have an issue with you. Just normal. "How are you?" Well, I have to be polite...

That's when I see her... She's beautiful, even without make-up. Her Brazilian weave really suits her face. You can tell she just had a baby, but she looks healthy and happy. She gives me a cordial smile. I guess she doesn't know who I am, and you take the cue.

"Baby, this is my old friend, Onome. We went to school together..."

*Wow... What an intro.* Maybe you would fill in the other part about how we were once an item and madly in love later... Or maybe that is not how you choose to remember us.

I swallow some saliva build up in my mouth. I am instantly aware that I could have looked better. I really didn't try with my make-up today, and I still haven't done my hair. I have to get to the salon today!

In keeping with good manners, I give her a friendly smile and extend my hand. "Nice to meet you..."

I realised then that you never mentioned her name. Am I supposed to know? Believe me, I'm not a stalker! Apart from that brief time that I was looking for you on social media, when one of your friends celebrated their birthday, you really never cross my mind... And I never bothered to learn about your bae either.

"Moyo," she volunteered. "Nice to meet you too." I think I like her. That's not a good thing. Well, maybe it is. Now, I care how she feels... A little.

An awkward silence follows. I quickly take the opportunity to ask the question that has been bothering me since I met you again. "When did you move into the neighbourhood?"

"Last year," you say, and I nod. *Well, this is awkward...*

"Alright, nice seeing you..." I say and pick up a random item on the shelf to inspect, hoping you'd both disappear.

It was after you left that I remembered that I could have told you about my book! I don't know if you or your wife read much, but I'd be keen to know your thoughts on my story. Maybe you'll relate. Anyway, I think it was seeing your wife that made me lose my confidence... Everything I thought I would say if I ever saw you again just flew out of my head, just as I wished I could run away...

I quickly finish my shopping, pay for my items and return to my car. I see your car parked outside the supermarket, and upon checking the number plate, I confirm that it was you parked at the Church the other day. *I think I need to relocate!*

# FOUR

So, I finally got my hair done. *Hmmm...big braids really look good on me. What a difference* 😁. I was so pleased with my new look, that I couldn't help but post some new pics on Instagram. Yeah, I was also kind of hoping you'd get to see them... Oh, well... I guess I will never know.

It's been a few weeks now, and I haven't seen you again. And it should be a relief. For a crazy minute, I thought you might even add me on Facebook again, but I should have known better. You've always been stronger than me. Always had the upper hand and control over me because when I loved you, I loved you with all of me...

I remember how my mom said it's better for a man to love a woman more than she loves him. That way, he'll never take her for granted. But I think the real doom is when there is an imbalance of love, either with the man or woman. I can't love less than my potential...and I don't want to be with someone who despises or penalises me for loving absolutely...or who holds back for fear of being hurt. That's misery.

Anyway, thankfully, life has resumed its normalcy since I saw you last. I can actually go days without giving you a thought. I don't even look out for you anymore. The pain of seeing you again has numbed almost to oblivion.

But the pain of being unhappily married lives with me still. Unlike a lot of unhappily married couples going through a turbulent or stressful marriage, where they know they love each other, and things are just hard or someone is behaving badly...I don't have that assurance that I am loved. In fact, it's knowing that I am not loved by my husband that is the root of my unhappiness.

Our problem isn't that we fight all the time. Our problem is that we don't talk to each other. We're not friends but strangers. We hardly have anything in common, and neither of us (as I'm also guilty) are willing to sacrifice or compromise to accommodate the other. It's like we can't stand each other. We are actually like two magnets that push away from each other, rather than attracting each other. And it's lonely and miserable and painful.

It's especially sad because I know all the right things to say and do, but I feel so hopeless because it takes two! He doesn't see a need to go for marriage counselling, though I've asked repeatedly. He seems to think the solution to our problem is for me to concede and even desire to have another child with him. But the thought frightens me to death!

Having another child with him will not make him love me anymore than he already does(not). It will not give us more time to bond or grow in love. It will come with its own sets of problems and financial burdens, and we're struggling already to look after our only child. The thought of bringing another child into this loveless marriage on the expectation that love will come with the child, that blessing will come with the child, that joy and everything else we ever wanted will come with the child, feels me with such a dread of bondage!

And what about the child that has become the pawn?! The marriage fixer. The one on whom our happiness will be hanged, and who will probably get the blame or feel like they were to be blamed for being the straw that broke the proverbial camel's back?! Rather than address and resolve our issues, he wants to deny and ignore them and proclaim by faith that the next child we have will be the boy he has always craved! Well, I do not have the faith - or should I say, *audacity* - to take such a chance.

So, I'm stuck. And it's scary, because I know something has to give. He has developed or, rather, maintained a habit of coming home late almost daily, and even sleeping out on occasion, in the name of work and Church! I don't trust him, but I've stopped caring about what he does or doesn't do. My only concern now is for our child, the beautiful girl we share. I just want her to grow up feeling loved and worthy, and never making the foolish mistakes I made...

My phone beeps with a new notification. Temi just sent me some messages on WhatsApp. *"Happy Valentine's Day!"* *"Sorry I forgot. Been busy."* *"Will try to come home for dinner."* *"What's for dinner?"*

*How romantic!* See what I mean?

# FIVE

I took my daughter to the park near our home today. She loves it there. She gets to play with the other small children and tries to be the leader! She just turned five, but looking at her, you'd think she's six years old.

Anyway, as I looked about the park, I remembered that last night we were together in London, when we visited the park near my University. Do you remember it? The memory of that night is dull now, but I remember the pain of letting go that I was feeling at the time, because I was still trying to hold on to you, when God had told me to forsake you.

That's sort of how I feel now... Just you coming back into my life has taken me back and given me a glimpse of how deeply I once loved and felt loved. And even though I know it's all a mirage, I don't want to let go of that feeling...

I remember also, one of the last things you said to me; that if I ever need you, I can call on you. Why did you say that? Since you said it, it's been an open door, a lifeline to reconnect when I find myself missing you.

But it doesn't comfort me...it torments me. Because I know that if I ever take you up on that offer, you really can't provide the help I need... You can't be who I want you to be. You can't even be my friend.

"Mummy, why are you crying?" I hear Lara say. I quickly wipe the tears off my eyes and cheeks. I forgot that she was there, and that she's so observant these days.

I smile and pull her close for a hug. "I'm fine dear... Are you ready for your dinner?" I ask, as I arise from the sofa.

"Yes, please. I want Indomie and egg." I smile at her predictable response, nod and respond in the affirmative.

I appreciate the space in the kitchen, as I prepare her meal. There's beans in the fridge, and enough plantain to fry for Temi, if and when he returns home to eat. I make enough noodles to share with my baby girl, as I am also cutting down on what I eat these days.

While cooking, I do what I have become accustomed to, I browse my social media accounts, particularly Instagram. And right there, as I open the app, I see a recent picture of you! OMG! That was so unexpected.

I quickly click the name on the account bearing your picture, before Instagram does that annoying thing of reloading the page with new posts so that you lose the one you are interested in. The account holder is indeed one of your close friends. He is celebrating you for your birthday. But that was about a week ago.

Yes, I still remember your birthday. I don't light a candle for you or anything. A few of my friends and even family members have birthdays and anniversaries around the same time, so don't let it get to your head.

Anyway, you're looking good. Not drop dead gorgeous, not like you've ever been. But attractive, regal and sexy, as standard.

I look through the comments, hoping to spot your handle as you say thanks for the greetings. There are quite a few of our mutual friends who have commented, but I don't see any handle that looks like yours. I decide to drop a comment anyway. I know I shouldn't. I should just move on..."waka pass" as they say. But the pull to get your attention is strong.

I write: "*Happy belated Birthday, Lade! Hope it was awesome :)*" and send it before I change my mind.

It was harmless... You'll probably never see it. But I know I shouldn't have. I feel the urge in my spirit to delete it, but before I do, I get a notification that our mutual friend, Ola, who posted the picture, liked my greeting.

It doesn't mean anything, I decide. And I leave that imprint, that reminder that we still share the same world…

# SIX

And then it happened. Trouble came knocking. But I was the one who poked the bear...

A couple of days after I dropped that message for you, I got a notification on my Instagram that Demilade Adetunji wanted to send me a message! OMG! To say my heart was racing would be an understatement. *Why* and how do you *still* have this effect on me?!

I must have looked at that notification for at least a minute, not knowing whether to accept or reject it. This was what I wanted, *right?* For you to get in touch with me... To let me into your world again. I was only curious.

But Wisdom said "NO". It was very clear, until my desire dulled the counsel of the Lord. What was the harm? It was only a greeting... Friends reconnecting. Of course, nothing would happen between us, because we are both married now... Not like before, when I was engaged to Charles and you were seriously involved.

But what about the pain?! Oh, I remember the pain so well. I know how long I grieved for you. How powerless I was over you. How *wicked* you were to me. Why should I give you the chance to make me weak again...sabotage my relationship with God and throw away the years of growth I've had without you in my life?

But it is true, as they say, that curiosity killed the cat... And I was a sucker for curiosity; for you. I closed my eyes, and let my heart decide and accepted your request.

"*Hey, you!*" you had written, so jovially.

A wide smile had spread across my face. *I hate you!* - My brain told my heart to believe, but my heart was deaf and blind to any warnings from my mind or spirit! It was soaring on a cloud, floating in weightlessness, caring for nothing but for the pleasure of this encounter.

I calmed myself down before I wrote "*Hi, Lade*". And then I fell back on the sofa feeling like a stranger in my body. I was falling again...with just a word from you and I was lost in desire and passion. *Are you the devil?*

You didn't respond immediately, so I clicked on your profile picture and visited your Instagram page. That's where a world of pain opened up to me! You had totally moved on... You had a wonderful life in the present, and here I was still stuck in the past.

Your latest picture was of your newly born baby boy, looking so cute and angelic in a picture-perfect, black and white portrait. It was posted over a week ago. There were more pictures of you and your wife, your family, friends, colleagues and business associates. There were also some inspirational messages you shared and others you reposted from other people's timelines, and I was surprised to see that they were deeply spiritual messages about God's love...

*What do you know about it???* So, you're now a Believer? *Saved?!* What took you soooo long, I thought in condescension and agony?!

I scrolled back to the top of your profile page and read your About message: "*Son of the Most High God. The Priest of my home. Letting my light shine for His glory!*"

"*Yeeehhh!!!*" I exclaimed, as conviction struck my heart. Your intentions were pure, and mine were not. I, who am the daughter of the Great King...a Minister of His Word, thought evil of you and didn't care to reach out to you to spread the love of Christ, only to feed my need...my flesh.

*Oh, God forgive me! Please take this obsession away... Please God! Help me to love this Brother and my Sister, his wife, with YOUR love... And God please...give me the grace to love my husband and build my own home. Amen.*

Moments later, I got a new notification of your response to me. I clicked to read it, my hands trembling. *Oh, wretched human that I am... Why have I put myself in this situation - again?!*

"*Thanks for the birthday greeting :) I saw it on Ola's post.*"

And that's when I thought, *why didn't you just respond to me there? What are you looking for in a private chat?* But the fact that you are now saved, a Believer, just like me, made me reconsider and believe that this re-connection was actually harmless. Certainly, your intentions were pure. And I was also reminded of the need to purify my heart, and bring every thought into captivity, submission and obedience to Christ, my Lord.

"*You're welcome.* ~~How was it?~~" I deleted the second sentence before posting my reply, because there's really no point fueling a discussion or relationship with you. God was right. I shouldn't have reached out to you nor accepted your offer to chat again. My heart is filled with more wickedness than I could ever know... Better to be cautious.

But you did not show such caution. You carelessly reached out to me as you wrote back; "*It's been so long... How are you?*"

Staring at the message, I yell in my mind, *God, what am I to do with this man?! Should I ignore his message and run away?* I ask the Lord. But He doesn't answer me; rather He leaves me to my own devices... And now, I'm in trouble!

# VOLUME TWO

*"Behold, all ye that kindle a fire, that compass yourselves about with sparks: walk in the light of your fire, and in the sparks that ye have kindled. This shall ye have of mine hand; ye shall lie down in sorrow..."*
(Isaiah 50:11).

## SEVEN

"*I'm fine... How are you?*" I reply.

There is no point in denying that I want to chat with you too. I want more, but chatting is all I can hope for. And I know that after this, this one opportunity, I may not get the chance to talk to you again, for a long, long time. But I don't for a minute imagine that you would want more from me too.

"*All's good :) I see you finally published a book! I always knew you would be a writer...*" you continue.

I am positively glowing now. I'm trying to think what would make you say that. Writing was a dormant passion of mine for many years.

"*Really?*"

"*Yes, of course. You used to write poems all the time. Do you still write poetry?*"

OMG! This guy... He's either a wizard or filled with the Spirit of God, I think. It is as though you know I have written a poem for you. I swallow hard.

"*Sometimes... As inspiration comes.*"

"*Ummm... Any inspiration lately? I'd love to read one of your poems 😁*"

*See me see trouble oh!* You cannot be serious. How could you ask to see my poems, just like that?

"*Nah! They're private.*"

"*Pleeeaaasssee... Or are they about me?*"

*You're mad*, I exclaim in my head! Lade, you're mad! What's all this? I am tempted to tell you the truth, even to show you the poem, but I choose to ignore you. I can't be that stupid!

"*Hmmm... I already told you, it's private.*"

"*Okay oh... Well, just wanted to say hi and thanks for the bday wishes.*"

I start to panic a little, thinking that you're going, and that will be it between us. God knows, I can't poke you again just to chat. Why am I missing you so much? Why does the knowledge of your happy life and your NEW LIFE as a saint not hinder me from wanting our OLD LIFE and love back? I need help! I need *deliverance*!

"*No worries. Take care of yourself.* ~~*Congrats on your baby, again.*~~" I scratch that last bit because there's really no need. You should just go back to the rock where you've been hiding! When I thought you were dead and gone and was free from the bondage of loving you.

Except, I now realise that I wasn't free. I thought I'd been free, but it was only as the magnet outside of your magnetic pull. But as long as you're alive, and as long as there's something in me that craves you, I am not free of you. I only enjoy temporary relief brought about by sufficient distance!

Right there and then, I think I need to block you. Take the control. Cut you off as you once did with me. Why should I suffer, when you do not even feel the same way towards me? Why should I endure this torment, just with the small hope that you may, once in a while, give me the pleasure of your attention?

"*I like your new hairstyle, by the way.*"

*Wow!* Where did that come from?! So, I see you have been checking out my page too. Now, I'm glad I uploaded those pictures...

"*Thanks :)*" I reply, smiling.

"*You should come out now and then. Everyone says you're scarce these days...*"

*Everyone?* Who's everyone? Who have you been talking to?

Does this mean, you still think - and ask - and talk about me?

"*Just been busy on my hustle... But I do go out sometimes.*"

"*Cool... Well, maybe I'll see you one of these days.*"

"*Yeah... Maybe.*"

"*We're doing my baby's dedication next Sunday. At Church and then at my house. If you're free, stop over.*"

"*Okay :) Thanks for the invite. Congrats again!*"

"*Thanks* ☺*!*"

But I know I won't. I can't. I shouldn't! God, please give me grace!

I pull out the poem I wrote for you a couple of months ago and read it again. And I know, I can never let you or anyone see this!

## **LOVE ADDICT**

I still want you,
With every ounce of me...
Seeing you again
Took me back to where we used to be.
Gone was the memory of all the pain,
Of the things you said,
Things you did and didn't do...
Only for the chance to hold you once again.
But alas, you're married with kids,
And so am I...
I wish it wasn't so,
But it is what it is.
We couldn't work before,
And we can't work now...
Yet, I am awakened to my need for you.
A wound is opened,
And the pain is real...
That you were all I wanted,
But all I couldn't keep.
Oh, how I wish our tale was different...
How I wish you had loved me,
The way I loved you...
How I wish you'd fought for me,

## PERFECT LOVE

The way I fought for you...
Looking at you again,
There are no tears to shed.
Only the realisation of my weakness,
Of my desire to be yours again,
To be yours at last...
To be yours forever...

# EIGHT

Like a moth to a flame, I find myself, on the day of your baby's thanksgiving, at your home! What the *hell* am I doing here?! It's as though I can't get enough of the pain! What kind of stupid curiosity is this? Is this really love or just craziness?

I'm happy to meet several of our old friends and school mates, who you are apparently still close with. You, always the social buddy, can't seem to shed your loyal followers. I, on the other hand, have found that my circle of friends has not only changed, but also greatly diminished.

I think it's also a man and woman thing... Too many things change in a woman's life once she gets married that it's really hard for her to keep up with her old friends and former life. We tend to get new friends, married friends, who are also friends of our spouse. Men, on the other hand, do not suffer such great changes, only the added financial and emotional burdens of marriage and parenthood. And of course, many are not shy nor hindered from meeting new women, or even keeping old relationships with their female friends, exes or not, alive.

*Hmmm...* Anyway, I can't help but admire your abode. I can't say it's humble. Like your car, it screams of wealth and prestige. It's also very tastefully decorated. Nice one.

There are several frames on the walls, some containing pictures of you and your wife on your wedding day and pictures with your families and of the children too, while a couple of frames contain passages from the Bible about love and marriage. I swallow as I read them. I really shouldn't have come here.

There are lots of people about, and Moyo is busy attending to your family and friends. You've been distracted with talking to your many guests since I got here about 30 minutes ago, so that you haven't even acknowledged my presence yet. But I try not to let that bother me and focus on the conversation I am having with Tobi, an old schoolmate of ours.

"Can you believe the audacity of Mr. President? To call Nigerian youths lazy?! That's just rich! I'm just tired of this country, abeg..."

"I feel you... It was terribly insensitive," I say.

"What about his own children? What work, what contribution have they made to this country, besides helping their father chop our money...money that can change the nation and put an end to poverty?!"

"Hmmm... Did you hear that they have been transporting strangers from Niger to register them to vote in Nigeria?! See rigging, Lord!"

"I heard that shit!" Tobi exclaims. "I read something about it on Instagram. This country...it is only God that will help us."

I notice you glancing my way now... I guess you're finally free to say "hello". My heart begins racing as you head over to where Tobi and I are seated on the sofa.

You arrive and give me a smile and offer your fist for what I can only imagine is a fist bump. I return your smile and connect with your fist, feeling torn about how to translate that greeting. It's so casual but yet so comradery. Tobi gives you his own fist bump, before you settle on the sofa beside him.

"So, what are you guys gisting about?"

"Naija my country oh!" Tobi says dramatically.

"Ah... I see. The youths don vex oh... 2019, the game go change... Let them just keep talking shit," you say, and I give you this look like "*I thought you were a Christian!*"

I mean, I do swear myself, on occasion... I just know that it's usually a big thing for Christians to swear, and I was already starting to put you on a pedestal of an exalted "man of God". Forgive me. That's really the only way I can make sure my thoughts towards you remain pure.

As the conversation goes on, and switches to sports, I make less and less input. I've never been much for small talk or gossip, and I have ZERO interest in football. Yet, I smile, say "hmmm", "yeah...", "really?" all in a facade to show I'm paying attention, but I can't wait for Tobi to leave, so you and I can actually connect...like we used to.

But I know that will never happen. In this place, I can only be promised your shared attention. It's too unrealistic and insensitive for me to expect more. And then I realise, I'm bored, and I've exhausted the purpose of my visit. It's time I start heading to my house.

Tobi's ready to leave too, so you decide to escort us both to the car park. Tobi is still chatty so, at the parking lot, I wave goodbye to you both before heading to my car. I thought I saw something in your eyes for a brief moment, but I'm sure it's only my imagination.

# NINE

I honestly didn't expect to hear from you after that. Especially that same day. It was your family celebration, and no doubt you would have been busy attending to your guests and catching up on some rest and quality family time later. Plus, you hadn't really shown any interest in my presence, anyway.

So, I was quite surprised to get a notification late at night from you.

"*Hey, Onome. Thanks for coming today :)*" you had written.

I looked at it, thinking it was too late to be chatting with you, and I should probably respond the following morning. But I succumbed to the itch to simply respond with: "*My pleasure.*"

I didn't really know what else to write. I put my phone down and went to make a cup of tea to drink in bed before sleeping. Lara had school the next day, so she'd already been tucked into bed. Temi had been home after Church until about 6pm, and then left for another event. I had no assurance that he'd be back that night.

I returned to my room and found my phone blinking with a new notification. After settling back in bed, I picked it up. I'd received some new likes on the post I'd shared on Instagram earlier that day, and a new message from you. After delaying to look through my notifications and respond to comments, I clicked to open our chat.

"*I didn't think you'd come...*"

*Uh? So, why did you ask me?* "*Well, you're my neighbour, and old friend. It's not like it was a trip or anything! Lol!*"

"*Is that why you came?*"

*Jeez! This guy has problem oh!* I swallowed some saliva build-up, wondering where you were going with that. I sipped my tea.

"*You invited me, nau! What, you thought I would be afraid or something? I'm happy for you, and I wanted to show my support :)*"

"*Thanks. It was nice seeing you again :)*"

"*And you. I'm glad I came. Met a lot of people I haven't seen in ages. Thanks.*"

"*Yeah... Maybe you'll be coming out more.*"

"*Yeah...*" I sighed. It seemed clear to me that you still wanted to chat, and to be honest, so did I. It was a nice change to my routine, having someone to chat with...and mostly, having *you* to chat with. "*So, I see you're now a Believer 😁 When did that miracle happen?!*"

"*Lol 😊 You haven't changed!*"

And so, we started talking again. And for a while, I forgot how much it meant to me, until I lived for the notification of a new message from you, and for those blissful moments we chatted when I knew you were thinking of me too. It seemed harmless, until I realised that I could no longer, I did not want to, live without you in my life.

It wasn't long before we began to reminisce about our past, and the powerful feelings we once had for each other. Even the plans and promises we'd made to each other. And the game changer for me was when you wrote: "*I think I'll always love you, Onome.*"

You don't know what those words did to me! Why do you continue to say such things? God, I'm right back where I was with you, and thinking that it could be mutual was both exhilarating and dizzying. We have to stop now before we crash...

And then the Lord ministered to me, in a poem. As He spoke the first words in my soul, I knew it was something I needed to write down. And I cried as I wrote every word, reminded of God's love and will for me...to choose life.

## CHOOSE ME

My child, why do you go to the desert in search of water?
You will not be satisfied in your pursuit for happiness,
For love and validation, except in Me.
Why do you look to man,
Whose thought every day is wickedness?
Why will you not rest in Me,
Lean on Me, trust in Me...walk with Me?
I will lead you to streams of living water,
Where the sun's rays do not burn,
Where the air is nourishing and sweet,
And your whole being is at peace...
Choose Me. Do not be deceived by the enemy...
He will take all of you,
And your sorrow will know no end...
He will never finish consuming you,
Though you will wish and cry for an end...
There is no end to his torment,
Just as there's no end to the joy I promise...

# TEN

It's been three weeks since that night we reconnected, and I think I'm going crazy... You do not only plague my waking hours but my sleeping ones too. My dreams feel so real that my body still burns when I'm awake. And I spend my days looking forward to the nights when I can feel your soft, full lips on mine, your hard hands caressing my body and your heat inside of me, as you make love to me.

I lay in bed now, recalling my fantasies and knowing that the deed is done. I am an adulteress... It just hasn't happened in the physical yet. But you're all I want and live for, and the thought of never having you again makes me wish for a swift end to my misery.

I've rediscovered my love songs collection, and today I'm listening to Gloria Estefan's greatest hits. So many of her songs remind me of different times in our relationship. But the one that speaks of now is "Here We Are". It seems like the song was written for us, and I can't get enough of it, so I put it on repeat.

Where are you now? What are you doing? Are you thinking of me? Dreaming of me too? Or is this a self-imposed delusion?

I feel like a fast train, out of track and heading for a collision that even God cannot and will not stop. My only question is if I will survive the collision, but I know I can't get off this track... It's too late for me now. I do not even have the strength to pray for the grace to survive.

Do you know that today's my wedding anniversary? Temi didn't come home last night and he just sent a text saying that he has some important engagement tonight... He says we will go out for dinner on Saturday to celebrate. Six years of marriage. What are we celebrating?

I pick up the phone and call you. I can't help myself. I need to hear your voice. I need to talk to you. But you do not answer my call.

I go to the mirror and stand looking at the woman there. I do not recognise her. *God, what has happened to me?* Where did I go wrong? Why did I marry this man? Why can't I abide by my calling and bear my cross with faithfulness? *Please save me from myself...*

I go to the bathroom and wash myself. I freshen up, dress up, style my hair and put on some make-up. I try to smile at my reflection, but I know even if I deceive others, I can't deceive myself. Still, I try.

After picking up my daughter from school, I return home and put her down for a nap. I'm glad she's already asleep, so I can work on the article for the online magazine I write for. I need to submit it by Friday. You see, after Lara was born, I gave up my job as a marketer to focus on building my career as a writer, which is something I can do flexibly from home. Aside from the magazine, I also work freelance as a copywriter. It doesn't pay much, but it's my passion.

I'm just done with the article, when I get your notification on Instagram.

"*Hey, sorry I missed your call... What's up?*"

I'm elated that you contacted me back. I quickly save my work, before settling to chat with you.

"*It's my anniversary today...*" I don't know why I told you. I guess I just needed someone to tell...

"*Oh, congrats :) Doing anything tonight?*"

"*No. He has to work. So he says...*"

"*Hmmm... Okay.*"

"*Sorry... Was just feeling like I needed someone to talk to...*"

"*It's okay. Are you home?*"

"*Yes...*"

*"I'm heading to your street to see a client. I can stop by."*

My heart is positively racing. I feel like begging you to, and to hurry up too, but I know it will be a disaster. I don't even want you in my home... It's really not in a state I'm proud of.

"Oh, thanks, but... I don't think it's a good idea."

*"Oh, okay. Well, we'll be at The Prestige Suites... If you want to come over. We can talk."*

I swallow hard. That's a new hotel on my street. The idea of meeting up is so tempting, and I wish I was stronger, but I know it's all I been longing for.

*"Cool :) Thanks. Let me know when you're there."*

I fall back on the sofa, my heart galloping with anticipation and excitement. And I know I'm finished.

# ELEVEN

My stomach was in knots as I walked into the hotel. You'd sent a message saying you were done with your meeting, and that I should meet you at the Lakeview Lounge on the third floor. I'll admit, I went to redo my make-up, and chose a different dress for the occasion. Lara had woken up by then, so I left her in the care of my house help.

At the lobby, I was shown the way to the lounge, and wondered why you'd chosen it to chill, instead of the restaurant downstairs. You were sitting on a sofa, engaged on your phone when I entered the small, empty lounge area. You looked up at me and smiled, and something in me jumped for joy.

*So, here we are...* Face to face. And the last thing I want to do is talk.

You open your arms wide for an embrace and I almost rush into you. Oh, Lord, I've missed this. I've missed you. I've missed us.

Standing in your arms, I'm taken back to sixteen years ago when I loved you with everything in me, and you loved me too. That was before we separated only to meet five years later, in a different place, both taken. But it was only I who was still in love with you... The tears flow before I know what's happening. Then you squeeze me so tight, as if you also wish that I could enter you.

I look up at you, and you're looking down at me, and for a

moment, we're just admiring each other's face. Time has been good to you. You're even more handsome than I remember. I look at your lips, those thick lips that used to bring me such pleasure. And instinctively, my mouth opens.

The next thing I know, your lips are on mine, and you swallow them into your mouth, before releasing them sweetly. We kiss again, forgetting everything. Why I came. Why we shouldn't do this. Why we can never be together. There's no remembrance of anything except for the fire that burns between us.

Eventually, you pull away from me, and you're trembling. "Onome, I can't believe you still do this to me..." you say, and my heart soars. I want to enter into your arms again and finish what we started, but you just hug me and whisper. "I booked us a room."

And I know it's going to happen. I am already ready for you. I do not have even the inkling to resist. I just swallow and smile into your face. *I'm yours, Lade.*

Our love making is so surreal. The whole time, I keep thinking, *I can't believe this is happening...* I can't believe you are here with me... Making love to me. I wish it'd never end. I wish we could have this forever...

And then it ends. I climax in your arms moments before you reach your peak and come inside of me. Then you collapse on me and I stroke you, enjoying being with you again, and wanting to fall asleep in your arms. But then you roll away and sit up on the bed.

"Lade, lie with me..." I whisper, reaching out to hold you again, but you rise from the bed, out of my reach.

You begin to put your clothes back on, and I start to panic. An awful dread falls on me, as I realise, this could be it. Would you ever want to see me again?

I am only comforted as I remember how intimately you just loved me, and how you'd told me that you hadn't been able to get me out of your head since that day you saw me at the supermarket. I know I am not alone in this. But why are you rushing away?

"I'm sorry, I can't!" you say, and it's a little harsh. Your expression has changed. "I have to get back to work."

I sit up in bed, my knees up and the duvet pulled up to my

shoulders as I watch you. I want to ask you if we'll see each other again, but I'm too afraid to be so bold. I rather choose to enjoy the pleasure and the memory of what has been.

You're all dressed now and looking at me. You look guilty, and I know it's because you love your wife. Maybe you even changed for her. And I feel bad, because I was the one the enemy used to make you fall.

You come over and give me a soft kiss on my lips. And it feels like goodbye. I wish I could kiss you longer, but you pull away and head for the door.

"I love you," I say, and it sounds desperate. You smile, open the door and shut it behind you. And the silence is deafening.

## TWELVE

Then you did it again. You blocked me on Instagram. I returned home that afternoon happy after our time together and I was aching for more. At first, I waited for you to contact me, but when it was almost bedtime, I decided to send you a message.

I didn't really know what to say, because I didn't want to get your wife suspicious or worried, so I made it casual: "*Hey, Lade. How was your day? Mine was great* 😁"

That's still the last message in our chat since you never responded to me. In the morning, I checked your profile, but your page never loaded. For a while I thought it was my network, until I got notifications from others and was able to browse other pages. But yours never loaded. And that's when I knew you'd done it again!

Lade, you'll never know the pain I felt at that realisation. That once again, you'd rejected me. That I still wasn't good enough for you to keep, to fight for... That our love and passion meant nothing at all to you. *Lade, how could you leave me again???*

That first day, I cried until I was sick. I couldn't do anything that day. I barely managed to get Lara up and dressed to school. All I wanted to do was call you, and though I knew I shouldn't, I still did. But you'd diverted my calls too. Sending texts would have been pointless. It was obvious that I was never going to hear from you again...*you coward!*

You *bastard*! You couldn't even say "Goodbye"! You couldn't even tell me why?! I loved you! I gave you everything! I would have done anything for you! Oh, Lade...what did I do wrong?!

It's now been three days; three long, agonizing days since I heard from you. And my tears have dried. My eyes are empty and my mind is depressed, for want of a better word.

I've been contemplating what I am going to do now. I feel drained of life, of hope, of meaning... Every breath is drudgery and painful, and I keep wondering if I can do it. If I can end it all.

Which way would I go? I'm too afraid of pain and suffering, so drowning, hanging and cutting myself are definitely out of the question. I don't know the pain involved in poisoning, so I do some research on Google for the best drugs or poisons to take for a swift and painless transition.

Apart from knowing that my family and friends will be disappointed that I took the easy way out, I am also afraid of what this means for my salvation. I've heard that people who commit suicide do not make Heaven...but I think of how I have already spat on God's grace, by fornicating with you. We committed adultery, Lade. Two counts of adultery...and I am only sorry that my surrender wasn't enough to keep you.

I gave up God for you, Lade! My love for you overpowered my love for Him...and now, I do not have hope of His grace...

I want to cry to God to help me...to save me from what I am about to do, but I already know I can't live without you. I tried it before and you still found me, and stole my heart again, only to cast it aside like it was trash. And the pathetic thing is, if you'd just call me now...if you'd just send me a text message, I'd run back to you! Lade, you have become my reason for living.

And so, I know Heaven is not waiting for me...whether I die here and now or suffer another decade of this miserable life without you. You've ruined me, Lade. You've ruined me.

It is only after I take the pills that the thought occurs to me that death may not have been the only way out of my emotional prison and miserable marriage. I'd never wanted to consider divorce because of my Faith, but now that I had thrown it away, maybe divorce was an option. Maybe I could have just left Temi and accept the defeat that I failed at marriage. Maybe, life would have been worth living with just me and Lara.

*Oh Lara…* Why didn't I think of her until now? I'm thinking frantically of what I can do to undo what I've just done. I want to stand up, but my legs are unresponsive.

I can feel the effects of the drug overdose already. My head is pounding and I think it's going to explode. My heart is racing, partly from panic and partly from the effects of the drug I'm sure. My heavy eyelids shut and then…

# VOLUME THREE

*"If we believe not, yet He abideth faithful: He cannot deny Himself..."*
(2 Timothy 2:13).

## THIRTEEN

Onome, I found your diary a few days ago. I honestly wasn't snooping, and I have never been interested in that sort of thing. I have enough going on to keep my mind busy, and a lot more worries than wondering what's going on with you. But, we hadn't been talking much lately. There's so much we haven't and cannot say to each other. And you've become someone I don't know and I cannot love.

Onome, you used to smile a lot and laugh out loud. You used to enjoy life and look after yourself. You used to believe in me and inspire me, and I learnt so much from you. But I don't know what happened, if it was something I did or didn't do that made you become this woman...

These days, you're grumpy and moody, loud and angry, bitter and sarcastic, and very disrespectful of me. I know I am not where you hoped I'd be, and I have not done many of the things I promised to do. Things just haven't happened for us the way that I - that we - hoped, but I still trusted God and I tried to believe. I tried to stay positive.

But it seems like you don't know how to bend...to adjust and adapt. You only break under pressure. You are brittle, and I have come to expect little of you. Things I hoped and expected in a wife, I can't demand of you... And I thought we were in this together.

Do you even know the kind of pressure I am under? No, you do not have a clue! I know we're from different worlds. You were pretty much born with a silver spoon in your mouth, while I was a hustler from my school days...working hard for every break, and not always doing things above board. In my life, being right and surviving were often on opposite ends of the spectrum. Yet, I strove and tried to demand more of myself, and build a solid character in the face of non-stop resistance and oppression.

And it's because of this character that I've kept on believing... That I kept on pushing. But it became clear to me that I was alone in this. You stopped caring about me, and well, I stopped caring about you too. Maybe you'd say it was the other way around. I can see why you'd think so.

We both handle things differently, and I am not always emotional or passionate about the things you are emotional and passionate for. We don't often see eye to eye on much either. But the least I hoped was that you'd follow my lead. However, you're so convinced you're right all the time. And I saw that I couldn't lead you... You had no need of me.

So, imagine my shock...my pain...at realising that you've been fantasizing - *obsessing* - about your ex-boyfriend!!! Onome, what is it you want?! Seriously! *What do you want?!*

Is he the reason you can't love me? Is he the reason I will never be good enough for you? Is he the reason you're so unhappy...that you want to throw away your whole life?!

What about God?! Do you even care what is right or is this the broken you...the one who gives in to weakness because you lack discipline, self-control, resilience?! You used to go on about the Cross, but I've been wondering if that was just a theory to you. Or maybe it only applies for others and not you.

I swear, I don't even know who you are anymore. I don't know what you represent. I don't know what you believe. I don't know what you are capable of.

Never in a million years would I have thought I'd come home and find you sprawled on our bed, dying of a drug overdose. Onome, that sight was sickening! It was horrid! It was pathetic...

I really want to know what drove you to do this. To be so

weak? To be so selfish?! What were you thinking?!

You know, for a moment, a weak, wicked moment, I thought *good riddance*! Maybe now I can have another chance at love. Because the truth is, if you could do what you did, without caring about us - me and Lara - then you don't deserve us!

If not for God, Onome... If not for God... I'd have left you there.

But God. God and His talk of love... God and His talk of forgiveness and redemption. God and His message of hope. Because of God, I did the right thing that evening, and rushed you to the Hospital, where the doctors gave you the best care.

They said you were lucky. That if I'd brought you even a minute later, you wouldn't have made it. But I knew it wasn't luck. It was God again... Messing with my happiness.

# FOURTEEN

Yes, dear... I am happy. I am finally happy after years of being miserable. Years of feeling like I am not good enough and can never live up to your expectations. Years of feeling alone in this marriage.

I met someone. She's beautiful and smart. She makes me laugh. She makes me feel wonderful, Onome.

She loves me. All of me. Just as I am. We keep thinking if only we'd met each other before I met you. *If only*...

I really tried not to get involved with her. I tried to focus on making us work. On making you happy. But, you just kept driving me away.

I have needs too, Onome. And it has been so hard to stay faithful to you. We've kissed a couple of times, but it hasn't gone beyond that yet. But I know God is gracious. He will never give us more than we can bear...even though I always wonder how come He let us marry each other, when we are clearly not meant for each other.

I love her. Onome, I am in love with her. And I want to be with her... Whatever happens between us after this. Just know that this thing you did doesn't change anything...in fact, it only made me love you less, as I have realised that you're no longer the woman I married.

I was actually going to tell you that Saturday night when I came home. I was going to explain to you over dinner why I think we should consider divorce, even though it is something we both agreed we can never do. But we also agreed never to cheat on each other...but here we are.

Isn't it ironic that instead of celebrating six years of marriage, we would have been discussing divorce? But when we have stopped talking about everything else, that's the only thing I feel I can talk to you about honestly. Dissolving our marriage.

We've done so many things wrong, and I'm tired of watching my life waste away. This cannot be God's will for us - for me. I've been praying about it, and I can't see any other way forward but to admit that we have failed and move on. Reading your diary, I am more convinced about my decision than ever. You never loved me enough for us to have stood a chance.

So, I just want you to know that when you come back from the hospital, I'll be moving out. Don't try to change my mind. And no, I don't believe any amount of counselling will erase the damage that has been done or bring love into this marriage. I thought maybe another child would help us bond, and I really wanted a boy, but I'm now glad that we only have Lara. I know you'll both be fine without me.

I'm not going to fight you for custody. I want - I NEED - a fresh slate, and I know you'll be happy to look after Lara on your own. You never needed me before anyway... Either way, I will continue to give you all the financial support you need and stay connected for Lara's sake. But I'm done with us. I'm done with this marriage.

"Why don't you go home and rest?" I hear Ese say, as she puts her hand on my shoulder. "You must be exhausted."

I look at her, and struggle to smile. She has no idea. "Thanks."

"Don't worry about Lara tonight. She can stay with us for a couple of days. You need a break," she says, smiling. And I remember why I like her so much. Your ever-thoughtful sister.

I nod and rise up. I wipe my face as I walk out of the hospital room. But I'm not going home tonight. There's only one place I want to be, and tonight, I'm going to give her everything I've held back from her.

# FIFTEEN

Mirabel is excited about me being finally free. We had a mini celebration last week, actually. It's also been six months since we first met each other at the bank, where she works as a cashier.

It was her smile that first drew me to her station. Then it was her professionalism and efficiency that stirred an interest in me. She also has the most fascinating laugh that makes her angelic face even more radiant than usual. I was hooked from that first day. She became my cashier, and then my friend.

She's the one I tell everything to. My pains and challenges at work. My hopes and aspirations for the future. We have similar interests and a shared sense of humour. She gets me. She's really amazing.

But here I am with you, still playing happy families, because you think now's not the right time to tell your family that we're over. Your sister's celebrating her fifth anniversary, and we need to show up for them, and not spoil their happiness, you say. However, I am reminded more than ever why I have never and will probably never fit into your family. They don't regard me as anything, because I'm still not financially accomplished. I'm your husband, but not one of them.

Your older brother, Ruke, who's not even married yet, is surprisingly the rudest. Does he think that because he's running your family business, which he is neither qualified nor trained in, that it makes him a better person than me? Because he can afford to drive flashy cars and go on exotic holidays, he looks down on those who have to work for everything they have and still look after dependents. And why does he keep asking us about number two, when he doesn't even have number one, or a wife for that matter?

"Onome, how far now?" Ruke asks, as he looks you up and down.

You give him a version of your plastic smiles that never reach your eyes. "We dey oh... How body?" you throw back, as you usually do.

"Body dey inside cloth," he replies, giggling as though he's made a really funny joke. I can't help the smirk that crosses my face. I quickly take a sip of my wine to disguise the expression, and nod in acknowledgement of his effort to strike a conversation.

Ese is looking as radiant as always. She's still a sight for sore eyes, even after having three kids in five years. And I can't but compare you two. No one will even believe you are twins! Or that you used to be the finer one 😁!

I know it's not really fair, considering how well-off Martin is. But you still have to give it to her; she makes an effort. With only one child and freelance work, you really could do better, Onome.

Everyone rises when your parents and your younger brother, Efe, arrive. Martin's parents and siblings, with their spouses, are also present to celebrate the happy couple. And happy, they are. I can't help but feel a little envious as I watch Martin and Ese laughing together after sharing an inside joke. We were never so happy.

*** 

It was actually a lovely dinner, without incident. I kept anticipating but was not too surprised that no one made mention of your attempted-suicide episode. The conversation shifted from marriage to babies to business to politics and then marriage again. You said very little throughout. Which, I suppose is a good thing.

We ride back in a usual, uncomfortable silence, with only the radio to drown out our thoughts. When we get home, you come out, and I drive off, before you feel a need to ask me where I am going. We both know now that there's someone else in the picture for me. There's no doubt about it, our ship has sailed. I only have a few more things to pack out of our home, before the divorce papers will be ready and served. And I will be free.

# SIXTEEN

You see, another thing I love about Mirabel is that she's a mean cook! She makes the best egusi soup I've ever had. In fact, there isn't a soup she can't make.

While you were in the hospital, I realised that I'd been suffering, Onome... Instead of missing your cooking, she had me eating a different delicacy each day. Correct woman, with proper home training. And these few days living with her have just been amazing... Damn, I really settled.

Today's her birthday, and we're going to the movies. For the first time, I'm going to go out in public with her, and not feel bad for cheating on you. Our divorce is almost through, and I am just waiting on you to sign the papers.

I really don't get what the holdup is about. Shebi you wanted to kill yourself because of some man? Because I made you so miserable, eh? Kuku sign the papers, let's end this thing...

We've arrived at the Palms Shopping Mall, and I'm feeling like my old self again; a proper gentleman. I go over to Mirabel's side to open the door for her. I know she likes it and appreciates it when I show her such courtesy.

She steps out looking smashing in a red-hot number, and I'm feeling like the luckiest man in the world. Damn, she's fine! I can't remember the last time you looked so fine. Five years gone and you still haven't lost your baby weight, as if you're the first woman to get pregnant.

Anyway, I'm feeling like a teenager holding hands with the school hottie, as we walk into the mall, making our way to the Cinemas. I can't but notice all the guys checking her out, and I feel strangely proud, and not at all anxious about being seen with her. I wonder if your friends will see us and tell you how happy I am without you... And how good we look together. I can just imagine your face, when...

"Hey, Temi!"

I stop for a moment to look into the face of the man calling my name. He's an old mutual friend from Church. I'd seen him checking out Mirabel but didn't really recognise him. And I'm surprised to feel a little ashamed. I wonder what he must be thinking...

"Hey, Chudi! Long time!"

"It's been! How are you?" he asks, looking from me to Mirabel and back into my eyes again. That deep questioning look.

"I'm great! And you?"

"Awesome!" He looks at Mirabel now, intentionally, and I know he is hoping for an introduction or explanation. He returns his gaze to me, when Mirabel leans into me. I guess he got the answer he was looking for. I can see he doesn't know how to phrase his question. "So, I haven't seen you in Church lately..."

"Yeah... Actually, I've moved." And that's the truth. Even though we stopped attending Church faithfully many months before. There's also no point in telling him that I haven't been attending another Church at my new home, because it's really none of his business. Anyway, I finally decide, for Mirabel's sake, certainly not for yours nor his, to introduce her. "Mirabel, Chudi."

Mirabel extends a hand and smiles her sensational smile. "Nice to meet you, Chudi."

"Nice to meet you," he replies, but I can tell he doesn't mean it. He looks torn. I almost feel like telling him we're divorced, but that's not completely true. And I don't want Mirabel to feel more uncomfortable than she already does. "Temi, we really need to catch up. Are you on WhatsApp?"

"Yeah... On my Glo line."

"Okay. Still the old one, then? Cool."

"Yeah... Later man!" We slap palms and pull each other in for a brief hug, before I walk on with Mirabel.

For some reason, I don't feel as carefree and victorious as I'd earlier been. I am reminded that no matter how happy I am with my decision, I will still have to deal with other people's perspectives and opinions. And I really don't care, or should I say I don't *want* to care...but I can't shake the thought that maybe I'm missing something important.

*God, I just want to be happy!*

## SEVENTEEN

That feeling stayed with me like an irritating bug, and I kept thinking about us and wondering if I was sure of what I was doing. Do I love Mirabel? Absolutely.

Did I love you? I think back then I would have said "Yes, absolutely..." too, but now, I think I was just infatuated. Not only by you, but by the whole package you came with.

Married to wealth should have meant a life of leisure and pleasure for us. But I never thought you'd be so indifferent when it comes to material things. I mean, who quits their job to become a writer? I know I thought it was a good idea at the time, but I also thought we'd get more assistance from your family. But five years later, and we're still hustling and waiting on that "big break". And you wonder why I work all the time. Well, money doesn't grow on trees, Onome! Aside my nine to five, I still have to run a side business just so we can make ends meet. But it seems you don't have a clue.

Anyway, I know that it takes more than love for a marriage to work. And in that sense, I am a little hesitant with Mirabel, because I don't want to make the same mistake I made with you. I don't want to rush into marriage because of love or because of all the things I think she can offer me. This time, I want to be 100% sure. I want to know that I can't live without her for the rest of my life...

And unfortunately for you...and for us, that is now my gauge for deciding if I can ever return to you. I am so tired of being in a miserable relationship and marriage, just because divorce is a sin or adultery is a sin. I dread the thought of living another minute...even another second like that. I want to live breathing the free air and feeling thrilled to be alive. And I want to know that I am choosing to be with whoever I am with - 100%, because I know I can't bear the thought of being without them.

So, when Chudi sent me a message on WhatsApp, I felt like I could answer him, and didn't imagine that our discussion could leave me in so much more turmoil.

Chudi: "*Hey, Bro. Free to chat?*"

Me: "*Yeah... Wassup?*"

Chudi: "*I was just a little concerned about you...and Onome. Are you guys okay?*"

Me: "*Yeah. We're separated. Almost divorced actually.*"

Chudi: "*Wow! That serious!*"

Me: "*Yup. Pretty damn.*"

Chudi: "*Are you okay? You're taking it rather lightly...*"

Me: "*What do you expect me to do?*"

Chudi: "*Look, I know it's none of my business, but...you're my Brother. In Christ. And I know you both. I'm really quite bummed to hear this...*"

Me: "*It's okay. I understand. We tried. Six years...*"

Chudi: "*Six years is not forever. You promised forever... What happened? I hope you don't mind...*"

Me: "*Well, til death do us part...*"

Chudi: "*You're both alive, aren't you?*"

Me: "*Does attempted suicide count?!*"

Chudi: "*What?! Did you? Or did she try to kill herself?*"

Me: "*Yes, she did. So...does that count?*"

Chudi: "*Mehn! This is deep! What happened?*"

Me: "*I don't know... I guess she was unhappy. Does it matter? It was a pretty selfish thing to do...*"

Chudi: "*Yeah, I can understand that you'd be angry about that... And I'm so sorry that things got that bad between you two. But, yes, it really does matter why she tried to kill herself. You need to talk to her about it...and forgive her too.*"

Me: "*Look, this has gone beyond that. She didn't love me... She was still hung up over her ex. I don't know what happened between them, but I think*" he had something to do with her suicide attempt. She didn't even think of our daughter. I can't be with someone that selfish..."

Chudi: "Oh... There is another man in the picture. How do you know?"

Me: "I read her diary while she was in hospital. Look, I'm cool, alright? Thanks for reaching out."

Chudi: "Please...don't rush away. This is important. If you're not comfortable chatting like this, maybe we can meet up. I just feel a real burden for you. I need to know that you're okay and still hanging on to God through this..."

Me: "I'm okay."

Chudi: "What about God?"

Me: "I don't know."

Chudi: "Hmmm... You can't go far without Him, Temi. Your wisdom will only take you so far..."

Me: "I love Mirabel. And I think it's better I divorce Onome than keep her in a marriage where either of us will feel like killing ourselves - or even each other - just to get out! I want out of this marriage, and I think God understands..."

Chudi: "So, you and Mirabel are really an item... Wow. I don't even know what to say..."

Me: "Don't worry about it. Thanks again."

Chudi: "Okay... I just think you need to remember your vows. For better or for worse. I think you need to remember how you felt when you said them, knowing that hard times would come. That's marriage. This is the worse, and with God, it can get better. I also think you need to step out of your perspective for a bit and consider what she may be going through. Remember that she's your best friend. You're supposed to be her best friend. You're supposed to care why she felt so miserable that she wanted to take her life. You're supposed to be there for her, through the good and the bad...no matter how selfish she gets. You promised to always forgive her. Please... Before you opt out with a divorce, pray."

Me: "Thanks. I hear you."

Chudi: "Please, don't sign any papers yet. Don't do anything finite. You really need to give this more time, prayer and, most of all, LOVE! You're not doing it just for her, but for you too. Divorce will ruin you, as much as her. But if you let God heal your marriage, you will both enjoy more years together - whole and happy."

Me: Sigh. "Okay."

Chudi: "*God is able, Temi! And I know I was supposed to bump into you yesterday. I'd been praying for you all that day. I dreamt about you the night before, so when I asked God for a meaning, He said to pray. And then I bumped into you at the mall... You could have ignored me tonight, or told me to leave you alone, but I know the reason you're listening is because God is still working on your heart. Please, Temi. Give Him a chance and try to work things out with Onome. Give her another chance because, as you know, we all make mistakes.*"

At this point, I am in tears, and I don't know how to answer him. I don't know how to try again, Onome. I don't know how to forgive you.

## EIGHTEEN

I didn't reply back to Chudi, and thankfully, he left me alone. But only for a few days. He later sent me an article about "Marriage and Forgiveness", which I was tempted to delete, because I was sure I knew all it would say. But out of respect for him, and for God, I kept it there, like a little thorn in my flesh or a life-line, depending on your perspective.

I just want to move on with my life. Why can't people just let you move on?! We are past saving now... Where were they when it mattered?!

And my lawyer said you still haven't signed the papers... This delay is making me think, and I don't want to think. I don't want to go back to that place where we were. There's no way it can be better than how it was. Not when I'm in love with someone else, and I now know you were or are too. So, why the hold-up, Onome?

Suddenly, as if by magic - or witchcraft - my phone rings, and it's you. You haven't called me in months! You normally just send texts or WhatsApp messages. I wonder why the need for the call today.

"I thought you should know that I'm in the hospital with Lara. She's fine, but I think she'd like to see you..."

"What's wrong?"

"It's malaria."

"Okay. I'm coming."

***

Lara's a little angel. Even sickness doesn't take away her shine. And I had to wonder if this illness wasn't staged. She's ever chatty and I realised that I've really missed her.

"Daddy, when are you coming home?" she asked and I looked at you, wondering what you'd told her about our separation.

"Don't worry about me, dear! You just concentrate on getting back home, okay?"

"Okay, Daddy. I miss you."

I hugged my darling child, as I fought back tears. This is so emotional. I never knew it could hurt like this. I wished I could tell her that everything was going to be alright, but I'm still struggling to fulfill the promise I made on the day we married. I'm not keen on making more promises just yet.

"I miss you too, Sugar!"

After she fell asleep, I prepared to take my leave, but remembered that we still had unfinished business. I settled down beside you on a visitor's chair instead. You were lost in thought, so I took a brief moment to admire you. You actually made an effort today. You wore a nice dress, with a little make-up, and a new hairstyle. Was it for me?

I sighed. "So, when am I getting the papers?"

"They're here," you said, and a mix of relief and anxiety flooded through me. I don't understand the anxiety. You retrieved an envelope from your bag and handed it to me.

I stared at it for a moment. Something didn't look right. I opened it to find the document shredded to pieces, before turning to you in anger.

"Onome! What did you do?!"

"I tore it up, Temi! I'm not signing any divorce papers."

I swallowed and just stared at you, feeling a mix of emotions, but mostly confusion. "Why? I thought that's what you wanted?"

"We don't always want what is best for us... Temi, I'm sorry for everything I did to provoke this. Especially for trying to take my life. It was horribly selfish of me, and I can't imagine how that must have made you feel. I know it's going to be hard, but I'm not letting you go without a fight! Please, forgive me and come home."

I just stared at you, unable to believe my eyes and ears! So many words rushed to my mind and rushed out again. I didn't know what to say... I just knew that this was God again! And until I pay attention to whatever He's trying to tell me, I'm not going to get the peace to leave this marriage for good.

I rose up and left you sitting there, without saying another word. I had some thinking - and praying - to do. And sometime that night, I read the article Chudi sent. It was a really good article, and just what I needed.

And it would have done the trick too... I was all set to forgive you and try again, until I found out that other thing you'd omitted from your diary... *Onome, how could you?!*

# VOLUME FOUR

*"If a man say, I love God, and hateth his brother, he is a liar: for he that loveth not his brother whom he hath seen, how can he love God whom he hath not seen?"*
(1 John 4:20).

## NINETEEN

Then silence... Like a vacuum. Like my ears are being sucked into my head. And then I'm falling. I just keep falling, afraid of when I'm going to crash, afraid of where I am falling to, afraid that I will never stop falling.

And then it stops. There is nothing. No sound, no feeling, no taste nor scent. Only darkness. *Am I dead?*

"*No, you're not...*" An answer comes from nowhere and everywhere at once. I spin around in the darkness, very afraid of a presence I cannot see and touch, only feel. I didn't utter a word, but You heard and answered me.

"Who are You?" I ask. My heart is pounding fast. I am standing on something, but I can't see it nor describe the feel of it. My eyes will the darkness to clear so I can see, but I am also afraid of what I will see.

"*The One who loves you...*"

My breath catches. How am I able to breathe here? Where am I? I still don't know who You are, but I think You must be God...and I am ashamed.

"I am not worthy..." I say, as I bow down. I can't see You to bow at Your feet, but I get down on my knees, and then lower, until I am lying down, crying. I know I should be in Hell... I don't know where this is. I don't know why I am here and not there... "Forgive me, Lord!"

I am praying in the Spirit. Words originating from a source I do not know. But I know that I am confessing my sins before You. Every last one of them. I can't stop speaking these words that break my heart. That make me ashamed to stand before You. That make me beg Your pardon. *Oh, Lord, please forgive me!*

"*You are forgiven, Onome. Rise up.*"

And as I arise, the darkness clears, like it never was. All around me is brilliance and beauty. The sight is magnificent. You are everywhere. Now I know. You're in everything around me. *Is this Heaven?*

"What is Heaven to you?" the voice is that of a man, and he is beside me. I turn and see an angel. He is dressed in a radiant white robe, the stature of a small giant. Much taller than any man I've ever seen, but not so big that I feel dwarfed in comparison. And he is beautiful.

I smile as I behold his face, and I'm filled with so much happiness. His eyes, like glass, have such depth and warmth. And the smile on his face reminds me that he is waiting for my response.

"I don't know... This...this feels and looks like Heaven. Or some part of it. I don't know what I was expecting."

"Hmmm... Eyes have not seen, ears have never heard, nor has it entered the heart of man, what God has prepared for those who love Him..."

Then I look at him and laugh with joy. I know he is telling me that he too has not seen this Heaven that I am asking of. And I remember the Scripture in Revelations, when John wrote about a New Heaven and a New Earth, and how all the old will pass away... He, like me, is waiting to see this New Heaven.

"But why? Why am I here...?" I wanted to say that I had sinned, and committed suicide, and was supposed to be in Hell, but even my thoughts couldn't condemn me. Every thought was wiped away with Your words to me: "*You are forgiven, Onome.*"

"Mercy. Have you not heard of it?"

I looked at the angel, whose loving expression hadn't changed. I wanted to understand him deeply. Something was still hindering my ability to understand.

"It is written: "*I will have mercy on whom I will have mercy.*" The Lord has chosen you and spared you for a better purpose. Soon, you will understand."

I sighed deeply and smiled. You still loved me. Regardless of what I had done. You'd called me and chosen me, despite myself. And even after all I have done to soil Your name, You have cleansed away my guilt and shame, and set me to stand in confidence before You. *Lord, I love You.*

# TWENTY

I wake up to find myself in a hospital bed, alone. And I feel immediate loss, because I am missing You already. I'm missing the serenity, the beauty - Your majesty!

Suddenly, I'm bombarded with noises. All sorts of noises. From the "beep beep" sound of the machine I am connected to, to the quiet buzzing of the light bulb, to the hushed voices of the people outside, steps in the corridor; everything has a sound. And it's almost deafening, as it steals the peace I once enjoyed in Your presence.

And then You calm me down, with a reminder that You are still with me, in this place. That I am not alone at all. I am just on an assignment...and I need to be here, to do Your will, until it's time for me to return Home to be with You, forever. And the warmth and joy return to my heart, and I just want to stand up and praise You in song and dance.

As I begin to remove the tubes connected to my body, a Nurse comes in hastily and prevents me.

"Hey, hey... Welcome back, Onome! Take it easy..." she says, calmly. And I see that she has a beautiful spirit, almost like she's one of Your angels, sent to minister to me. "How are you feeling today?"

"I'm fine. Thank you. Have you seen my husband?"

"Yes... He was the one who brought you in. You must miss him..." she smiles.

And all I can do is smile. Because it's not actually true. I wish it was true.

What I miss is what we could be. The dreams I had of living happily ever after, when we got married, which I've long since discarded. I miss the hope and promise we had at the beginning. But the truth is, my husband is now a stranger to me.

"What about Lara? My little girl?"

"I believe she's with your sister. They were all here last night... They will be so happy to know that you're awake now!"

"Thank you, Nurse...Ana," I reply, calling her name as written on her uniform. She gives me a sweet smile and records some information in her notepad after doing a couple of checks.

After a couple of hours and a session with the Consultant Psychiatrist to determine my mental fitness, I'm released from the hospital. I call Temi, but he says he can't come for me, as he is in the middle of an important meeting. I decide to take a taxi home. Lara will be at school now too, so I should have the house to myself.

So, I'm back to the place that made me feel so depressed with my life...and it dawns on me that nothing's changed! The only thing I've gained is the encounter with You, which I cherish, but which is quickly leaving my memory. I begin to panic, as I try to recall how it was in Your presence. I try to remember You and all You said to me, about Your calling in my life, and why I must return...

I wish I could feel You here as I knew You there... I wish my angel, Seth, or one of Your many beautiful angels was physically here to guide, teach and encourage me. Why is it so hard to abide in Your presence in this realm?

When You spoke with me then, I felt able, I was inspired and passionate about coming back to be Your light. But now I am here, I feel like a rock trying to roll up a mountain. I feel overcome, defeated and afraid. *God, please help me!*

*Do not be afraid, Onome. For I am with you always, even to the end of the world*, You whisper, and I feel Your Spirit move in and through me, and all around me in an instant. And I know that that has to be enough. Otherwise, how will my faith be proven...? And then I recall Paul's words to the Church at Corinth as recorded in the

Bible: "*For we walk by faith, not by sight...*"

You have called me to go and go I must. You have called me to love and love I shall. You have called me to surrender, and I will and do surrender all to You. I have died, and now You live in me. This life I live, I live for You, who died for me and saved me. And even in my marriage, I will live for You. Because I am already dead to me. Lord, let Your will be done.

# TWENTY-ONE

And truly, truly, nothing had changed. If anything, it was probably worse. Temi didn't come home that night...nor the night after. Considering my new resolve to fight for my marriage, I was seriously bummed about it.

I tried not to think that he was with someone else, though I'd suspected that he's been cheating on me for a long time now. I'd never found any conclusive proof, and he'd always denied it when I confronted him with my suspicions. But this was the longest he had stayed away from home. And this time it really hurt, because I'd only just returned from the hospital after a near suicidal episode, and he hadn't cared enough to ask me about it.

It was clear to me that he no longer cared about me, about us or even about his child. The least he would have done was call to see how Lara was doing. It wasn't until three days after I got back that he did just that, and only that.

On top of dealing with my own lack of passion towards him, I had to deal with my growing anger and resentment over his recent actions and inactions. I had to not take it personal and give him grace. I had to be understanding that he was probably acting this way because he was angry about my attempted suicide. But it would have been easier to believe that if he hadn't already developed this nonchalant attitude towards our marriage and established a Bachelor's lifestyle, such that his behaviour was neither uncommon nor surprising.

For the first week, I just kept going on auto-pilot and by grace. Praying constantly, choosing to be thankful and hopeful and faithful. I trusted in You and believed that things can only get better. If not, why would You send me back? Surely, Temi would come to his senses and realise that he is throwing his life and our love away and will come home without any push nor pleas from me, I reasoned.

So, I was dumbfounded the day he came home to gather some of his things, saying that he was moving out and was going to file for a divorce. I actually started crying. I don't even know where the emotions and tears came from. I was just feeling so emotionally drained and mentally weak. All I could utter was "Please, don't go!"

He'd looked at me then as if I was mad. I will never forget that condescending look on his face, filled with hatred and mockery. I immediately felt like I was fighting a losing battle and lost all the words I wanted to say. He couldn't care less about me, that was sure.

As he left with his things, I remembered that my sister was celebrating her anniversary the following weekend and decided to latch unto that to buy us more time to think things through. I begged him not to announce our separation until after their celebratory dinner, and he conceded. After that, I intensified my prayers and went to Church, where I made confession and sought more prayers and counsel. I immersed myself in You, and received strength to keep hoping, believing and serving in love. But Temi never came home to appreciate the efforts I was making to be a better wife.

We attended the dinner together, but I think it was obvious to everyone that we were falling apart. There was no intimacy between us. In fact, you only had to look for a minute to see the underlying animosity in the way we related to each other. Everyone was also aware about my recent suicidal attempt, and I was not really sure what to expect from them in the way of follow up. I didn't want to be a downer and bring it up, or even say anything to reveal that I was still feeling depressed, so I said nothing either, and tried my best to be jovial.

On the drive back, I wanted to tell Temi that I'd changed my mind. That I didn't want a divorce and thought we owed it to ourselves to try and work on our marriage. But every time I looked at him, he looked far away...and happy in some fantasy. There was someone else, that I was sure of now. And I knew he was thinking of her. I couldn't bring myself to say anything. But I was mad!

*God, this man doesn't love me! And I don't love him! Why must I stay? Why?!* I cried in frustration.

*Because I love him, Onome,* came Your still small voice.

In that moment, I recalled Jesus' words... "*By this all men will know you are My disciples, if you love one another, as I love you...*"

"Give me grace, Lord!" I cried aloud. "This is so hard!"

*I know, My child. That's why you must abide in Me. For without Me, you can do nothing.*

# TWENTY-TWO

It didn't get easier. I tried to focus on other things; my health and fitness, my work, my relationship with my family and Lara especially. I continued to pray for Temi and our marriage, and pray about my own heart and spirit. There were days in between that I was happy and cheerful, and moments that came suddenly, when I felt thoroughly depressed. Through it all, You kept me.

Funnily enough, the day I got the divorce papers in the mail, I was offered a promotion to become an Editor with the e-magazine, JV Magz, where I have a weekly column, "Living Free With Onome". I write on everything concerning life, love and Faith and usually get lots of comments and mail about my articles. The one I'd written a day after returning from the hospital had really gotten a lot of feedback, as I addressed the topic of suicide and depression, which, coincidentally, was a topical issue at the time.

Anyway, I'd actually just applied for a position as a Script Writer with their Media and Entertainment company, JV Media, and was even thinking they'd responded quickly. But the offer to be an Editor was still huge, and I was more than ready for the challenge. I was happy that my career as a writer was progressing, even though my personal life was disintegrating.

If not for You, Lord, I would have signed those papers immediately. I longed to sign them and to be free. But Your word through the Apostle Paul, kept running through my mind:

*"For he that is called in the Lord, being a servant, is the Lord's freeman: likewise also he that is called, being free, is Christ's servant"* (1 Corinthians 7:22).

In You I am both free and bound. I am bound to love; to be long-suffering, gracious, hopeful and kind. I am free in that the Law does not constrain me...only to submit and surrender to Your Spirit and Your will. And I knew already what Your will was... The question was would I trust and obey or give up and do things my way. Well, I'd tried the other way, and it hadn't worked. I would try Your way.

I owe my life to You, Lord. I am living for You, Jesus. And I want to show Temi the unconditional, unrelenting, fervent love You showed me. I just need Your help every single day with it.

As I looked at the papers, I knew what I had to do. I had to rip them up, lest I be tempted in a moment of weakness to sign and send them. I had to destroy them, because divorce wasn't an option for me. In this marriage, I am Your servant.

Well, some days later, Lara got ill. I thought it was the usual common cold and treated her with paracetamol and cough syrup for a couple of days, but her temperature continued to soar. I eventually had to take her to the hospital, where they tested her and found out that she'd contracted malaria. As she struggled to take oral medication, she had to be hospitalised and treated with continuous intravenous infusion.

It was sad seeing her ill and bedridden. But what was sadder was that she kept asking for her father. She hadn't seen him in at least a couple of weeks. He seemed to have forgotten her, through all this, and that made me angry. He really wasn't making it easy for me to love him... But God, You told me to call him, and so I did.

When he strolled into the hospital room that night, I was surprised to behold his broad, fit frame. He looked so much better than I remembered him, and I found myself feeling weird about that. I was angry with him, yet, found myself so attracted to him in that moment. He greeted me curtly, and I returned his greeting.

I watched as he reconnected with our child, who was so happy to see her daddy. As I watched them catch up, I felt a knot in my heart. It was a sad realisation of what we could have been. A happy family. All I knew was that I wanted that, and if it was still possible, I'd do anything to have that dream...that life.

But when he came to sit beside me, I remembered the other obstacle to our happiness. I could smell her on him, and my heart broke. Yes, I can't believe it...my heart broke! *When did I start loving this man?!* Or is this just a case of wanting what you cannot have? Coveting what another woman is appreciating...? *But he is mine*, I said to myself jealously! *He is still mine!*

When he asked after the divorce papers, I felt a little defiant and triumphant to give him the envelope with the shredded document inside. From somewhere deep inside, I found the desire to fight for him. It was like the desperate instinct to survive, when you're on the verge of dying. And I rode on it as I told him...begged him to come home.

## TWENTY-THREE

To my utter surprise, Temi came home the next evening. By then, Lara had been released from the hospital. I'd opened the door to find him looking tall and rugged, and immediately felt my heart skip. He gave me a brief smile, before entering with the oversized teddy he'd bought for her.

Lara ran into his arms excitedly, and for a moment, I worried that his visit would be brief. He wasn't carrying any luggage, so there was no way of knowing his intention. And then he turned and looked me square in the face before asking, "Anything for dinner?"

Wow, I can't explain the joy I felt at that request. I also felt anxious, since I wasn't prepared for it, yet I nodded quickly in response. I had some soup frozen and could warm it and make semovita within 15 minutes.

"Just give me a few minutes," I said with a small smile, trying to contain my happiness.

When I'd prepared everything and set the table, I announced that the food was ready. Temi rose up carrying a giggling Lara to the table. It was such a beautiful sight, to see how happy she was to have her daddy home. We haven't sat down together to eat at the table in at least a year, so this was really something.

I was so nervous to have him back, that I didn't even know what to say. I had questions, lots of questions. About where he'd been... Why he'd come... How long he intended to stay... If he was ready to seek counselling with me... But I just kept sighing, because I didn't want to scare him away or annoy him with my questions.

"You okay?" he eventually asked, and I saw care in his eyes.

I swallowed. "I'm glad you're home..." was all I could say.

"We've got a lot to talk about..." he said, and I felt unease in my tummy.

Something was happening. My prayers were being answered, and now my heart was involved. It wasn't like before when I wanted to care but felt nothing. Now, I cared too much. And I really wanted him to want me too.

I eventually got Lara to go to sleep, and returned to the living room, where Temi was watching a program on television. For the first time, I worried that he was still going to ask for the divorce, and that his coming was not really about us working things out after all. But at least we were going to talk. This was progress.

It was the longest time before he decided to mute the TV and turn to me. I waited in anticipation for him to say the first words. He leaned forward in his seat and met my gaze.

"Onome, why did you rip the divorce papers?"

I swallowed. "Because I want us to work..."

"Really? Since when?"

I closed my eyes, afraid to speak the truth, which is that it was truly a recent development. "Since I said "I do"..."

He smiled then, a sad smile. "Onome, you can't lie to me. You know, I read your diary..."

My eyes opened wide then, and I became instantly afraid that this won't end well. I tried to recollect all I'd written in it, especially my last entry. Whatever he'd read, I could understand why he'd struggle to believe my profession of love.

"Why did you...?"

"Please, save the guilt-trip. I read your diary, while you were in the hospital, after attempting to take your own life...and end our marriage! If I hadn't come home in time...we wouldn't even be having this conversation!"

*If you'd been home earlier...if you'd been there for me, we wouldn't be having this conversation either*, I said in my head, and struggled to keep it there. But the blame game was going to take us nowhere. The point was what we wanted and were ready to do now...

I swallowed. "I'm not mad at you for reading my diary. Like I said, I'm so sorry about what I did, and I pray you'll find it in you to forgive me..."

"It kinda depends on the why, Onome. Why did you do something so selfish? Was it because of him?"

I rested my face in my hands for a moment, as I tried to control my emotions, even as I recollected them. "It was because of a lot of things... And yes, he was a factor."

Temi looked at me then and asked me the question we both feared. I wish he hadn't asked and I wish I could have lied to him. I knew it would make everything so much worse... But it was inevitable that he would ask, especially after reading my diary.

"Did you sleep with him, Onome?"

I cried then, as I nodded. All the emotions rushed at me suddenly, but the greatest was loss. I felt like I had just shot myself and killed our chance at reconciliation.

I was surprised to see tears roll down his cheeks. He refused to wipe them, nor answer my pleas, as he made for the door and left me alone again. *God, what had I done?*

# TWENTY-FOUR

Hypocrisy. They say that is when you demand from others what you do not expect of yourself. Faithfulness. Fidelity. Love. In this regard, we were both hypocrites.

Yet, I was ready to forgive. Even though he had moved away from home, and in with another woman. Even though he flaunted their relationship before me and the whole world, shaming me, our marriage and our Faith. Even though he hadn't repented of his sins...I had forgiven him and was willing to take him back.

It was easier to be gracious to him because I knew in my heart that it could have and would have been me, giving my heart and body, even soul to another man...if he'd so desired. I am here alone primarily because of Lade's rejection, not because my love for Temi or You was superior. I am here now, because of Your amazing grace that pardoned me, cleaned me up and purified my heart... Now, I stand, not simply as one loving with the will, but with my heart...and that is nothing but the grace of God.

It hurts more now, than it did before. My heart is tender now, and I've shamelessly given it to Temi...the man to whom I pledged to love for better or for worse, before I knew what love was. It hurts that he doesn't love me back and will not forgive me for my betrayal, even though every minute of every day he is betraying me by living with another woman. But who am I to talk?

I would, but I no longer have the liberty to do as I please. Nor do I have the heart to rebel. Every day, I long for his forgiveness and, ultimately, his repentance and deliverance. *Lord, when will You arrest him like You did me?!* I don't know what else to do, especially when he will not come home... *God, what am I to do?*

The days go by and I do not hear a new word from You. Only the assurance that You are still with me, and that You're working everything out for the good of all. So, I abide in Your love. I abide in the knowledge of my call to love, as You love me. I am secure in the knowledge of my identity in You, as Your child and Your minister. I know I can do all things through Christ who strengthens me...

***

It's been a week since Temi walked out on me. He's been home a couple of times since, but only to check on Lara and spend some time with her. Each time, he avoids looking at me or being alone with me, and I keep wondering if we'll ever get to say the things we need to say to each other.

I decide to seize the moment today to confront him on his hypocrisy. He doesn't deny it, nor does he repent of it. Instead, he says, selfishly, "I'm tired of being miserable, Onome. I forgive you, but I can't stay in this marriage anymore." And then he hands me a new set of divorce papers.

I look at the document, my heart burning within me, as I curiously flick through. I am shocked and mortified that his grounds for divorce is *my* infidelity! HYPOCRITE! I swallow hard and pray for grace.

I feel like giving in and giving up, but at this weak moment, You come and help me and give me the words to say...

"Temi, I will sign these papers on the condition that you give us a month. In that month, you will return home to live with me, you will eat my meals every night, and we will sleep in the same bed, at the same time. We will attend marriage counselling every week and pray together for our marriage to work."

Temi is looking at me dumbfounded. He wants to say something, but I interrupt him, by putting up my hand.

"I will never sign these papers until you give us a chance! If you have truly forgiven me as you say you have, then you will make this last effort, for us...for Lara, for *God*. If after this month, you still see no hope, then I will sign your divorce papers. That's my condition of acceptance."

PERFECT LOVE

# PART TWO

"*And above all things have fervent charity among yourselves: for charity shall cover the multitude of sins*"
(1 Peter 4:8).

# VOLUME FIVE

*"...if two lie together, then they have heat: but how can one be warm alone? And if one prevail against him, two shall withstand him; and a threefold cord is not quickly broken..."*
(Ecclesiastes 4:11-12).

## TWENTY-FIVE

Sitting in the waiting room of the counsellor's office, waiting for and wondering if Temi will show up, I close my eyes and travel back in time as I recall how we got here. How did things get so bad that we need a mediator to have an honest and loving conversation? My memory is not what it used to be, but still I try, because I know it will come up at our session today - if Temi shows up.

I remember that I was still emotionally and spiritually unstable at the time Temi came into my life. Though it had been years since my shameful fall, I still hadn't gotten over it. It had had such an impact on my self-image and esteem, because before then, I'd always considered myself to be a good Christian woman; loyal, faithful and trustworthy. I was engaged to one of the few decent guys left in the world. And he loved Jesus with all his heart.

Charles wasn't romantic or charismatic as Lade had been. He wasn't sexy or even very attractive. But he loved Jesus and he was a virgin! And he cared about me a lot. Yeah, I never really felt *loved* by him either. We lacked…chemistry, but we were friends.

Though Lade hadn't been my first love, he had been my first sexual partner. And I had fallen so hard for him. Because of my Faith, because I knew what we were doing was wrong, I had to give him up. But the damage had already been done.

I think Lade left a hole that no one else could fill… So even though I was moving ahead with plans to marry Charles, for many good reasons, as I believed love would grow, I still had one eye open, waiting for something to happen to change my course. And that something manifested as Lade.

It was crazy how it happened. I actually thought I'd gotten over our first break up, until I saw him again. And like a pack of cards, my whole world crumbled.

Lade and I carried on a brief affair, as I tried to convince him that we were made for each other. But he said he was serious about his girl, and eventually dumped me without warning. I'd been depressed and love-sick for months, and it was obvious for Charles (and anyone really) to see that he wasn't the one I wanted and I wasn't his better half either. He'd called off our engagement and moved on. A year later, he married my best friend! It's weird how I didn't see that coming.

So, when Temi came into the picture, I was still nursing all sorts of insecurities, and felt quite unable to and unworthy of love. I found myself making the same mistakes I made with Charles…entertaining a relationship simply because someone thought I was "the one". I doubted that I'd ever meet or fall in love with someone who would love me the same. It was hard enough to even find a good Christian and *celibate* brother, not to mention one who loved me and was ready to marry me.

The truth was I was spiritually and emotionally immature. And I was tired of waiting for love…and for God. So, I said "yes" to his proposal.

Unlike my relationship with Charles, we did have chemistry, and sometimes, it felt like love. But it was really lust. Though we were abstinent, we kissed and did other things that ignited the fire before time. So, that also clouded things for me.

Even though I thought it was too soon and things were moving too fast. Even though I was beginning to see things about him that I wasn't sure I liked and was beginning to have doubts, I ploughed on. I didn't want to lose another Charles. But if only I'd known that marriage is no play affair. It's no joke at all.

The foolishness of what we had done, entering a marriage

without godly wisdom and counsel, or even without real love for each other, became apparent to me once we added a new member to our fold. The pressure of life, working to look after the family, paying medical bills, school fees etc just magnified our issues.

We disagreed a lot. And in the course of our frequent disagreements and constant unhappiness, we'd said things to each other that we never should have... Like "I hate you", or even worse, "I don't love you". I found my escape from the emotional pain by channeling all my focus on Lara, while he chose his work, Church and friends to escape to. And that's how the gulf became wider and wider.

I tried to bridge it often, and I know he tried too, but we were always out of sync, and our efforts were half-assed at best. We had so many issues, trust being a primary one for me, and it just seemed easier not to want more...than to keep fighting for a dream. It really was only a matter of time for everything to fall apart...

I really can't say it was one thing or a few things we did in our marriage that led us here. I just think our foundation was all wrong, and we'd never taken the time to correct it. Yes, we both believed in God, but He wasn't Lord of our hearts, our marriage nor our home.

*Hmmm...* I sigh and look at my phone for the time. It's about ten minutes past the time of our meeting now, and I am beginning to think Temi won't make an appearance. I decide to call him, and then I see him, as he strolls in lazily. *Thank God he came.*

## TWENTY-SIX

"So, Onome has told us her reasons for having these counselling sessions. But I think it's important we hear from you, Temi, and understand the purpose you hope to achieve from this..." the counsellor smiles and looks pointedly at my husband.

Temi moved back home a few days ago, at the start of the month, and this is our very first session. After finally choosing a counsellor, the next challenge was fixing a time to meet. Finally, we settled for Wednesdays at lunchtime, but he'd remained pessimistic about the outcome of the sessions. So, I am certainly eager to know his response to her question. He looks very uncomfortable, and even angry or annoyed. It is hard to tell which exactly.

"I want a divorce..." he finally says, looking back into her eyes squarely. I swallow.

That was not a surprise. He's been resolute about his goal in all this, which is for me to realise the futility of my efforts and sign his freedom papers. I really hoped and believed God that he'd make an effort, but it seems like the more I try to show him love, the more he tries to prove that he is unlovable.

"I see..." the counsellor mutters and writes something in her pad. "So, do you think there's a possibility that you could change your mind...?"

He shakes his head. "We've been married six years. There's nothing that can be said in four sessions to change what has happened. I'm afraid this is just too little too late..."

I am looking at the counsellor, wondering how we are going to proceed from this. How can we have a counselling session when one party is uncooperative? How can we have a marriage when one party is determined not to have one?

"Do you want to know what I think?" she asks instead, and I sit up straight, because I am interested to know.

A muscle ticks on Temi's temple as he clenches his jaw. "Not really... But go on," he says.

"I might be wrong, but I think perhaps you're afraid..."

"Of what?"

"Well, that's what I want to know... Maybe you're afraid of failure... Or even success?"

Temi rolls his eyes, and I look at the counsellor, thinking she's losing him. "What kind of a therapist are you?"

She simply smiles. "Second chances can be really daunting...because you feel like you've been there before and done those things at a time you were at your best and should have succeeded. It is normal to be anxious after failure, to try again...especially when you are feeling inadequate and discouraged. It takes a lot of faith to have another go and believe that this time around, you will get it right...that you will succeed.

"Whatever the obstacle was before, it appears bigger now, scarier... But we often forget that we are much more equipped now than when we first began. You have experience, understanding of your unique strengths, weaknesses and differences, and hopefully, more wisdom. Giving up is easy. But it takes courage to give it another try..."

I smile and look at Temi. His face is expressionless.

She straightens up and speaks matter-of-factly. "Okay, I understand that your full and genuine participation in these sessions is the condition on which you will get what you truly want... In order for you to know, and for Onome to know, that you cannot truly fix your marriage if you try, you will have to give 100% to *trying*. Otherwise, I'm afraid that you would have proved nothing...except your willfulness to have your own way...even at the expense of your own happiness. So, can I just suggest that you change your focus for the time being to align with the real purpose of these counselling sessions, which is to discover the issues hindering true intimacy in your marriage and figure out how they can be overcome, so that you will have the marriage and the life you both desire?"

Temi swallows and shifts in his seat. "I don't really have a choice, do I?"

"You do, actually," I speak up, at last. "Fixing our marriage is your choice to make. God knows that I cannot force you to do anything. I am only asking you to remember your vow to me, to stick it out for better or for worse, so that you can fight for us. I am asking that you give priority to our marriage!

"Throughout our marriage, you've given priority to so many other things, and now that we have finally realised the need to save our marriage, you are saying it's too little too late. It's not too little. And it's not too late. I'm still here...and so are you. I am ready to give this all I've got if you will too... But I cannot save us on my own."

# TWENTY-SEVEN

The session ran smoothly after that, and I was feeling rather optimistic. Overall, I thought it had been a fruitful session. We shared our perspectives on what we felt was the problem in our marriage, what we believed needed to be done for things to change positively, and ultimately what we were willing to start doing differently to make our marriage work.

The bottom line came to accumulated resentment and unforgiveness. Because we had gotten into the bad habit of not talking about issues that upset us, there was a mountain of things that together seemed impossible to forgive and overcome. One thing the counsellor said, that really struck a chord with me, was the need to *trash* everything, rather than thrashing out everything, to move forward. She explained it like the way God forgave all our sins...past, present and future.

He didn't have to pick them out one by one to decide whether or not to forgive. With reconciliation as the goal, He choose to forgive all and even forget our sins and give us a whole new life in Him. Without His absolute forgiveness, we would always feel condemned if we fell short in any way, thinking that it will add to the reserve of unforgiven sins, and take us beyond the threshold for mercy. But God does not keep score with us. He continues to give us grace and forgive us, and that is the only way we can love each other.

It doesn't undermine our sins and their impact, it only exalts what we value more; love, joy, peace, grace and fellowship. Like they say, "*love conquers all*"! It actually recognises our weakness and our desperate need for an assurance of love and fellowship, regardless of our worthiness, so that by this pardon, we can respond in love and gratitude. What He has shown to us, is what He has demanded of us... Just as Jesus said, if we will not forgive our brethren when they sin against us, then we shouldn't expect that we will be forgiven.

So, it was no longer about who started it. Who did this or didn't do that. There was no more need to point fingers, because there was no option of measuring mountains. Whether our offences were the size of a mountain or a molehill, they required the same absolute treatment - to be trashed. To be forsaken and forgiven. And then we were both on the same level, neither condemned and both accepted.

It was really a huge relief of burden to have that discarded. To not have to fish through all the issues and assign blame and responsibility, so that one party would be feeling defensive and another justified. We were both guilty and were both justified by our decision to forsake the grievances of the past and choose to face the future together. This time, ready, willing and able to grow in love.

Without our offences clouding our vision, we would finally be able to see the good in our union and build on it constructively. Even without being madly in love, having sincere love and respect, without bitterness, should have yielded positive fruit in our marriage. The problem was we wanted love, but we didn't *practice* love. We didn't give love to each other, and so unforgiveness and resentment quickly built up, making our lives miserable.

I think Temi was pleasantly shocked with how the counsellor handled the situation. I know he'd been afraid that he'd end up being the target and getting all the blame for our failing marriage. He'd been initially resistant about having a woman counsel us...and worst of all, a woman *I chose*.

However, she'd come highly recommended by the Church, with a really good track record of restored marriages and homes. Her service was also free, though we have the option of donating towards her ministry when we have completed the process. I think that was what tipped the scale for him.

As we drove home together, my shoulders felt lighter and the air smelt fresher. I felt clean, like the way one feels after a really good cry, even though I hadn't cried. And I felt hopeful, with a new bout of faith about our marriage and future together.

The only thought that bothered me was the realisation of the desperate wickedness of man, even to turn God's grace against Him. For many insincere, grace becomes a license to live untransformed and unrepentant lives, as to be expected of those shown mercy. The thought of Temi using this grace against me by continuing to do what he had done before, because I am bound to forgive and love him unconditionally, troubled me. I knew I was sincere...but I wasn't a 100% sure that he was...

Then the Holy Spirit reminded me of His perfect love...which is without fear of abuse, because it is no longer concerned with self, but with the object of one's love. We give love because that's what they need and keep hoping and believing that the power of love will prevail over every heart. I then recalled and chose to meditate on Paul's definition of love, and prayed for more grace to love Temi that way...

*"Love is patient, love is kind. It does not envy, it does not boast, it is not proud. It does not dishonor others, it is not self-seeking, it is not easily angered, it keeps no record of wrongs. Love does not delight in evil but rejoices with the truth. It always protects, always trusts, always hopes, always perseveres. Love never fails. But where there are prophecies, they will cease; where there are tongues, they will be stilled; where there is knowledge, it will pass away..."*
(1 Corinthians 13:4-8).

# TWENTY-EIGHT

Things improved slightly after that. We both made more effort to communicate and be civil, but we were far from being affectionate and tender. Even though we shared the same bed, we slept on opposite sides, as though there was a third person in the bed.

The issues were still there. The things I found annoying about him hadn't miraculously disappeared, and I imagine it would have been the same for him too. However, we both tried to be more gracious, respectful and understanding of each other. I tried to reduce my expectations and demands of him, and just appreciate whatever he was willing to do and give freely. Including his time.

The truth is, you can force someone to be physically with you, but you can't force them to be mentally or emotionally with you. Yes, Temi came home every night, which I appreciated, but his mind wasn't really present. If he wasn't entranced by the television, he was engaged on his phone or laptop, watching all sorts of videos, sending endless messages and basically keeping himself entertained without including me.

Thankfully, the counsellor had given instruction for us to go on a date this week before our next appointment. It was a compulsory assignment, from which we would share lessons at our next session. I was looking forward to it, and we'd fixed a day and time. At the appointed time, Temi hadn't returned home, and my calls weren't going through.

I was getting nervous, thinking maybe he'd decided not to continue our efforts at reconciliation, when he sent a text message saying that he was on his way. I was too happy and nervous to ask him more questions, like why was he late? Where was he? What time will he be here? I was just glad that he was choosing to take me out, because it was still his choice to make.

For our first date, Temi opted for a movie, which was starting a few minutes after he got home, so we were rushing to make it. It really wasn't the best. I'd been dressed since and made up, but he thought that I was overdressed for the Cinema, so I quickly changed into a top and jeans, but kept my heels on. He slipped out of his suit and pulled on an old pair of jeans and t-shirt. It wasn't romantic nor attractive, but at least, it was us together, out and about. It was a nice change.

On our way going, his phone vibrated with a call where it was stationed connected to the car charging point. I could see the caller ID - Mirabel. *Was she the one?* Why was she still calling him? I looked at him wondering if he would pick up the call, but he just ignored it, until the ringing stopped. Then a text came in from her. It flashed on the screen, and with my eyes already trained on his phone, it was easy to read her short message before it disappeared: "*Hey boo, lunch was great! Missing you xoxo*".

It was a sure evidence that he was still doing his dirt and this was all a big joke to him. For a long time, I tried to keep it to myself, thinking that it would make no difference, except maybe to make matters worse. But as he parked at the Cinemas, I couldn't help but say something.

"Are you still seeing her?"

He looked at me guardedly, hesitated and then admitted it. "Yes...but..."

I put my hand up to stop him. "Please take me home."

"Onome, it's not like that..."

"Please, just take me home. You don't want this. You're not taking this seriously. God, I can't believe you!" I cried, despite my resolve not to.

"Onome, please, can you just let me explain...?"

I sat back and closed my eyes, thinking nothing was going to make it okay.

"Look, things got really serious with us...and well, she doesn't understand what you and I are doing and why I'd shut her out. She came to my office today and we had lunch, and I explained to her that I needed to give 100% to this for yours and my own sake...so that I will know that you and I are truly over, before we will have a chance at building real love," he swallowed. "I swear, nothing else happened. Well, she kissed me, but nothing else happened."

I didn't even know what to do then. I didn't know what to say either. I just swallowed and thought we'd missed the movie already. I just wanted to go home. I wasn't feeling this anymore.

"Onome, I'm sorry..." Temi said sincerely, and instinctively, I rose up from the passenger seat.

"Thank you." I looked in his face, and he gave me a small smile. He was trying. That was good. At least he was trying. "Do you mind if we watch something else?"

"No problem... But we'll probably be waiting 30 minutes or so..."

"I guess, we'll have to find something else to do while we wait," I said, and smiled timidly.

To my surprise and pleasure, Temi reached out to hold my hand, and I let him. So, we walked into the Cinema together, choosing to spend the evening with each other.

## TWENTY-NINE

"So, how was your date?" the counsellor asks, looking between me and Temi.

We're both smiling today. Temi nods and mutters "Good," and I do the same.

"Great. Where did you go? Did you have a chance to talk?" she prods.

"We watched a movie," I say, and notice her raised eyebrow. "But, we had a drink at the bar while we waited. It was nice."

She nods and turns to Temi. "That's good. I'm happy your first date went well. Next time, I'd suggest something more interactive, that will get you guys talking, learning more about each other, and even working together. It doesn't always have to be dinner or a movie. There are lots of options out there. And I hope you will share more about it when we meet," she says, smiling.

Temi and I exchange a look and return her smile.

"Today, I would like us to focus on romance, and its importance in nurturing love in a marriage," she begins. "Temi, would you consider yourself a romantic guy?"

He shrugs and nods.

"Onome, would you agree?"

I look at Temi, before deciding to answer. "Ummm... Sometimes. He was a bit romantic at the beginning."

"I see... Why is that, Temi?"

"I think I am pretty romantic... I just don't think I need to keep it up, with all the other things I have to do. I mean, there are more important things in marriage..."

"Actually, you'd be wrong..."

My jaw drops slightly, before I close it quickly. I see Temi's expression has changed to the way it is when he is no longer interested in a discussion. I can understand his objection, because I'm not sure I agree either.

"What do you think of this scripture: "*Guard your heart with all diligence, for out of it are the issues of life*"? That's Proverbs four verse twenty-three."

I respond, "I think it means that we should be careful what we let into our heart..."

"Temi?"

"What she said..." he shrugs.

"Okay, well the heart is a central part of a man (and woman). Not only biologically, but spiritually. It is easily conquered, and when it is conquered, the person is easily overcome with all sorts of sins. Jesus taught that the things that defile a man originate from the heart. Chief of these sins is idolatry. That's because who or whatever takes possession of your heart becomes your central focus in life. So, God is very concerned about our hearts, and wants us to be diligent in keeping it pure and devoted to Him...

"In respect to marriage, the equivalent sin is adultery. In marriage, you give ownership of your heart to your spouse, such that they have your pure devotion, which is acceptable and blessed by God. But, when you do not guard that possession, but give way for another to take possession, you have committed adultery, even without the physical act of sexual immorality, which often follows from there. So, Jesus taught on adultery of the heart, and said that if anyone looks with lust at another that isn't their spouse, they are guilty of it. Are you following me?"

We both nod, and she continues.

"The heart, not our physical hearts, is commonly regarded as the seat of our emotions. It is the drive of a man and can be even more powerful than his will - that is his mind. The heart is actually the control tower of a human being... When you have the heart, you have the person.

"So, when God talks about establishing a new covenant with His people, He talks about giving us a new *heart*, and one that is of flesh and not stone. The kind of relationship God wants with us is one that flows naturally, from our hearts and desires. When He is enthroned in our hearts, He will rule our minds and every other part of us. But we can't serve Him with our minds, while our hearts are distant from Him. Jesus even said He hates such worship.

"Contrary to popular thought, love isn't merely an act of the will (or mind). It must originate from the heart to be true; and true love always births obedience. That's why Jesus said, "*If a man loves Me, he will obey My commandments…*" Likewise, it is in your best interest, Temi, to win your wife's heart, so that her love for you will originate from her deepest part, and you will have no problem with her submitting to you in love… Hmmm… I see you're interested now," the counsellor says, noting the way Temi shifted in his seat when she mentioned submission.

"You are both probably familiar with Paul's letter to the Ephesians, where he talked about husbands loving their wives as Christ loves the Church, and wives submitting to their husbands as unto the Lord. Which comes first?"

"Love…?"

"You're right, Onome. And not just any type of love. The Christ kind! Temi, can you describe the Christ kind of love?"

Temi swallows and then says, "It's unconditional…"

"And…"

"Ummm… Pure…" he swallows again. "It's humble. It's servant-like…"

"Yes!!! Thank you for that. It's *submissive*. Jesus modeled submission for the Church, His *Bride*, to *imitate*. It is also *romantic*…"

I smile, because I now understand, but Temi is looking confused by the reference to romance again.

"God's love through Jesus Christ is the most romantic love ever. So, Jesus said: "*For God so loved the world, that He gave His only begotten Son, that whosoever should believe on Him, will not perish, but have everlasting life…*" John three sixteen! That's powerful!

"Let me describe Christ's love for you. While you were yet

unworthy sinners, with NOTHING to offer Him, God loved you, and decided to humble Himself, come down to your level and relate with you, and teach you and lead you, and ultimately die for you...so that you will have the courage and grace to do the same thing...which is love Him in return. John wrote that "*we love Him BECAUSE He first loved us...*"

"So you see, we are not able to love God, without knowing what true love is...and so, He needed to show us and He did that in the most practical way! And then He asks us, not only to love Him back but, to love our brethren also. He said, "*this is how everyone will know you are My disciples, if you love one another, as I have loved you...*" John thirteen, thirty-four.

"So, Temi, you're going to have to do the same thing. You're going to have to chase and romance your wife... Not just in the beginning, but *constantly*. That is how you will guard, not only your heart, but hers too, and keep and secure your marriage from the sin of adultery. And your wife, when her heart is conquered by you, will be surrendered and submitted to you. You will *lead* her, not by force of will, but by her heart, which is devoted to you. Do you understand now?"

Temi nods.

"So, today, our focus is on how you can practice romance and cultivate love in your marriage, and how you *must* imitate Christ in modelling submissive love. Because that's really what romance is. The romance of a man courting a woman is him humbling himself, serving her needs, exalting her as queen, and seeking to fulfil her desires... And you should know, a woman in love will do *anything* for the man of her heart. You love first, and submission will follow."

# THIRTY

It was a really good session with the counsellor, and by the time our hour was spent, we'd learnt so much. She'd talked about love languages, something I'd read about before, but never really understood. But as we explored our different love languages, we were able to understand why there was so much misunderstanding and miscommunication between me and Temi. While I liked a display of love with outings, dates and gifts, Temi felt he was showing his love by all the ways he sought to provide for us and meet our needs. Likewise, Temi actually preferred words of affirmation, appreciation and love, while I pushed him for more time with me, doing the things that I felt were romantic.

We explored other ideas for spending our time and money on each other, in a way that honoured our values and need to minimise spending. However, I liked how the counsellor emphasised the importance of generosity, when it comes to spending time and money, because Jesus taught that "*where your treasure is, there your heart will be also*". We had to consider our regular expenses on things we thought we needed, but which were actually stealing from us, such as the amount spent on our Satellite Television subscription, which ended up taking up our time too! This is because we often felt we had to watch whatever was being shown, rather than using the time to talk, play or even go out together. It was a real eye-opener for me, and what was good was seeing that Temi was actually appreciating the session too.

We also talked about the need for building intimacy, through honest, constant and effective communication. The counsellor made a distinction between quantity and quality, when it comes to our fellowship. I realised that it's not about being together all the time, but about how intimate we are ALL THE TIME, whether or not we are physically together, so that when we are together, even doing different things, we still have quality fellowship and intimacy. The key is to build trust and foster a caring environment, where we both feel loved, safe to be ourselves and at peace.

This week, our assignment, in addition to going for a *romantic* (yes, emphasis on 'romantic') date, we had to do without our television, internet and social media, and go back to the basics. We had to learn how to talk to each other or be still and quiet in each other's presence. We also had to learn to do things together, including playing games with Lara. I was really quite excited and nervous about these changes, especially forsaking our TV programmes. I was just glad that we had the PVR to record what we would be missing, so it was like a holiday from the Television.

I am really impressed with how Temi is handling all these changes. Since our second week and first date, he hasn't complained about the counselling sessions or about anything really. He's more introspective and sensitive in the things he says. He's also been more thoughtful too, and even offered to do the dishes once this week! It was the day our house help was on leave, and I would have done them, but he said he'd do it. I guess without having TV to watch, he had time to do other things more helpful, I'd thought to myself as I smiled and left him to it.

For our date this week, Temi took me to a new Eastern restaurant in Victoria Island. Well, it was new for us. Everything about this date was miles better than the last. Temi arrived home on time and changed into something smart. He also had no problem with my chosen outfit, which he complimented, much to my delight. And to top it all off, he brought me flowers!!! It really set the tone for the rest of our evening.

Sure, our conversations still left much to be desired. We were not pretending to know nothing about each other, so we didn't build our conversations on questions and answers about each other's lives and aspirations for the future. We talked about what married people talk about; their kids, work, finances and the few friends they still share in common.

However, towards the end of our meal, Temi told me about Chudi, and how God had used him to reach out to him. It was because of his influence, that he'd agreed to come back home and work on our marriage. *Thank God for Chudi!* I'd said it aloud too, and Temi had given me a grin and a wink, to which my stomach had fluttered.

I longed to tell him about my heavenly experience too, but I felt the Spirit hindering me. It wasn't yet time for that.

# THIRTY-ONE

It was our fourth week together, and third counselling session, and I couldn't believe the progress we'd made. Yes, it was what I'd hoped for, and even believed God for more, like a miracle transformation... But, there was also a part of me that doubted that this 30-day challenge I'd given Temi would work. Realistically, we'd go the four weeks of marriage counselling, learn a lot of theory, and see little change in our lives...

However, things were really changing. We were both trying and growing and enjoying our marriage again. And I now wanted us to work so desperately.

Then it dawned on me that maybe the changes were not going to be enough to convince Temi against divorce. We still haven't had sex. Not that I am not keen on it, but he hasn't even tried... And we haven't talked about it either... Come to think of it, I don't think we've had sex - with each other - this year!

"So, how are you both feeling today?" the counsellor asks.

I'm suddenly nervous, being bombarded by my insecure thoughts. I give a small smile, and Temi smiles and nods. "Fine, thanks," he says.

"How did you get on with the new rules and ideas for spending time together?"

Temi is quiet now. I swallow, as I respond. "It was good. Challenging at times, but I think it was a pleasant change for us..." Temi nods.

"Nice. It will be challenging, especially in the beginning. But when you change your priorities, and give more time to the things that matter, your life will be all the better for it. Good job, guys! I'm really happy with the progress you're making."

I smile now, encouraged, thinking I'm not the only one who thinks there has been progress. Temi just nods, and I wonder what he's thinking.

"Okay, I'd love to hear about your date..."

Temi turns to me, as though in expectation that I'd speak. I smile as I say, "It was great. Romantic. We went to dinner at a nice, new place in the city." The counsellor is nodding, but still looking at both of us expectantly. I swallow. "I think we both had a good time."

"Yes, it was nice. We had fun," Temi adds, which makes me feel better.

"Alright..." the counsellor says, looking between us and smiling, before noting something down in her pad. "So, today, our focus will be on the expectation on the wife to submit to her husband as unto the Lord. It should follow naturally, when a husband is submitted to the Lord, and is showing godly leadership as modeled by Christ."

We both swallow but keep our eyes on her.

"However, it is important for you to know that because you are already married, Onome, and have pledged to follow your husband, you will need to humble yourself and submit...even when he isn't showing godly leadership. By that I mean, you can't be standing waiting for him to humble himself before you do. You also have been given the call to love your brethren as Christ loves you...and that is regardless of their worthiness.

"Remember, Jesus washed all His disciples' feet, even Judas', who He already knew would betray Him. By this, Jesus taught us to give unconditional, submissive love to one another. If your husband is not ready to lead the way in loving submission, you can and should, as one who knows the love of God and is submitted to Him."

I nod, but I'm not smiling. I really want to know where she's going with this...

"That's why Paul gave the teaching in First Corinthians Seven that even if a Christian woman is married to an unbeliever, she shouldn't seek to divorce, but must show herself a minister of God's love in that home. A Christian man *will* lead the way in love and submission, in obedience to Christ. And a Christian woman *will* submit herself to Christ and show loving submission to her husband. Do you understand?"

We both nod, and exchange a look, before returning our attention to the counsellor.

"So, Paul's teaching to the Ephesian Church about love and submission in marriage is really for both husband and wife to heed, because *both* are called to love one another as Christ loved them, and *both* are called to submit to one another. The emphasis on women to submit to their husbands, as unto the Lord, is to denote order and leadership in marriage. A man submitted to God leads... But if the man is an unbeliever and the woman is Christian, *she* leads in love... An unbeliever can't lead in marriage, because they have not known, nor are they submitted to the love of God. I hope you have a better appreciation of this teaching..."

"Yes, thanks for clarifying," I say. Temi shifts in his seat. I can tell he's still processing what the counsellor has said.

"Any questions, or objections, Temi?"

He shakes his head. "I guess I'd always thought that men are the leaders because, well...we are men. But now I see it's more about the Spirit of God; Love..."

The counsellor gives him a brilliant smile. "That's great... The authority is in love. I'm glad we are understanding ourselves."

Temi turns to me and smiles. And now my anxiety is gone. God is in this. We are going to make it through.

# VOLUME SIX

*"Therefore as the church is subject unto Christ, so let the wives be to their own husbands in every thing. Husbands, love your wives, even as Christ also loved the church, and gave himself for it..."*
(Ephesians 5:24-25).

## THIRTY-TWO

"Do you know what submission is?" the counsellor asks, looking between both of us.

"I think it is when you surrender control to a higher authority..."

She nods. "Yes, Onome."

"When you trust and obey..."

"Yes, Temi."

"When you humble yourself and put the other person before yourself..." I add.

"Good! You guys get it. Do you know what it is not?"

We both keep our eyes on her.

"Well, submission is not oppression. It isn't self-neglect or self-endangerment or self-hatred. By submitting to someone, you do not deny your own worth nor demean who you are. You can think about it in respect to Christ. Though He was God, He lowered Himself to assume the form of a man, but He was still God. So, submission doesn't change who you are, but allows you to minister to others without regard for it.

"This is very important because many men have misunderstood the concept of submission to oppress their wives and rule over them. But remember what Christ taught about leadership in His

Kingdom... He said that we are not to rule like the kings of the Earth, but that "*the greatest shall be the servant*"! So, in the Kingdom of Heaven, leadership is about *serving*, not about controlling..."

I'm smiling widely now, feeling relieved. But I also know that the call to serve, to ministry, to humble submission won't be easy. I have Christ as my model and my vision...and He went so far as laying down His life for me. I take a deep breath and utter a silent prayer for more grace.

***

On the drive back home, I'm deep in thought. Today's session was both enlightening and challenging. I learnt that the major hindrance towards love in our marriage is me - myself and I!

In so many ways, I am still trying to preserve me; who I am and what I want. I've been trying to preserve my way, my opinions, my dreams and my expectations. I have been afraid to die to self, but that is the only way I can live for Christ, and bear the fruit of love...

I am reminded of Jesus' teaching that "*unless a grain of wheat falls to the ground and dies, it abides alone, but if it dies, it bears much fruit...*" (John 12:24). Practically, Jesus was talking about His sacrifice on the Cross to redeem all of Mankind, and He said that for me to be counted among His disciples, I must deny myself and bear my own cross too. And it's becoming clearer to me that THIS IS IT... And on this cross of my marriage, I can't escape death...

We discussed what it means in practice, and for many, the practice of submission in marriage would seem objectionable. It would seem like going back in time culturally, because the concepts of human rights, justice and equality all get overthrown for humility, mercy and sacrifice. When you practice a perfect love that knows no fear, that is long-suffering and still *believes all things*, all you have is "*faith, hope and love...*"

"You okay?" you turn and ask me. I look into your face, and it's sincere. I smile and nod. "That was quite full-on!" you say, with a chuckle and a sigh.

I sigh. "Yes, it was. I now see all the ways I've hindered us. I don't think I ever really got the vision of us... Marriage was about me being loved, being happy, being fulfilled... Even saving our marriage has partly been about saving my reputation!"

You nod, as you turn your gaze back to the road. "I understand. I've been the same way... It's good to know it's not too late to change." You smile and look at me, and my heart melts for you.

"Thank you for giving us another try..."

You reach out and take my hand and squeeze it. "Thanks for believing and trusting God, even when it seemed hopeless."

I smile back at you, and rest in my seat, as we hold hands all the way home. This time, when you drop me off, you follow me to our doorway and pull me into your arms for a hug. I hug you with everything in me. Then you pull back, lift my chin up and give me a sweet kiss.

"See you tonight..." you say, as you rush back to your car, and leave me staring and longing after you.

# THIRTY-THREE

I was fully, and eagerly expecting your return home early tonight. I just suspected that maybe you would be interested in reconnecting with me sexually, and I made myself ready. I could hardly concentrate on much else all day, except to reminisce on the kiss, and what it symbolised and begin to dream of our tomorrows.

So, I was quite disappointed when you texted to say you weren't going to be able to make it home for dinner. Lara was in bed and I was already feeling sleepy when you got in after ten pm. And naturally, I was upset. Just when I thought we were making progress, it seemed like you'd taken another step back.

But to be fair, I didn't know what the issue was. All I knew was that since you agreed to move back and come home for dinner every night, this was the first time you'd returned home this late. I tried not to let my disappointment show, but the fact that you didn't see the need to apologise beyond the text message you'd sent, annoyed me.

With a sulk on my face, I'd opened the door to you, and mumbled that your dinner, which I'd spent time preparing with love and anticipation, was in the microwave. I knew I should have owned my emotions, I should give you some slack, because you're trying...but I'd really gotten my hopes up, and your behaviour tonight, just made me doubt our progress again.

"Thanks, I'm starving!" you said, but I couldn't see the

expression on your face, as my back was already turned to you.

I went to the kitchen to warm the food. Egusi soup and poundo yam, your favourite. When I returned, you had the TV on and were settled on the sofa, your shoes kicked off and laying untidily on the floor, while your suit was strewn along your favourite armchair. *Deja vu!* It was like we'd gone to the past. This wasn't progress! What about having the TV off so we can relate?

"Please bring it over here... I'm so tired, I just need to relax," you said, as I was already laying the food on the table. I could barely contain my annoyance.

"I thought we aren't supposed to be watching TV anymore?"

"*Huh?* I thought that was just for last week?"

"No... I think it's supposed to be until things are better between us, at least for this month..."

"You *think?* Well, *I* think we're good...and I'm tired and need to unwind..." you said, looking at me pointedly.

I returned to the kitchen to get a tray and brought your meal to you. After laying it down on a stool, I sat on the sofa and tried to calm down. It wasn't a big deal, I told myself. You'd obviously had a busy day today. *Just be cool...*

"*Hmmm...* This is nice!" you say, and the corners of my lips rise in a small smile at the rare compliment of my cooking. "Are you okay?" you asked, giving me a quick side look, before turning your gaze back to the TV.

I sighed deeply, a little pleased that you'd noticed and cared enough to ask, but still irritated because the TV was far too loud.

"Well, actually...I'm not. I was thinking maybe we'd talk tonight... I guess I'm just disappointed that things are already falling back into the old pattern..."

"*Oh, no...* Not again, Onome."

"Not again, what?!" Okay, now I was annoyed. *Are you really going to try to flip this on me?* I wondered.

"You're always blowing things out of proportion! Can't I just come home and relax? I sent a message saying I was going to be late..."

"I'm *always*...?"

"Okay, maybe not always... But you know what I mean..."

"No! No, I don't know what you mean. I don't *always* blow things out of proportion, but when you say things like that, you nullify my own experience. I thought we had an agreement. You were supposed to give us priority this month and come home in time for dinner... You didn't even tell me why or say sorry or anything!"

You sat up, turned down the volume on the TV, and rested your head in your hands, as you took some deep breaths. "Onome, I'm trying! I have a job, and responsibilities at work... And they don't prioritise my marriage! They don't really care about my personal issues. I thought because we were making progress, and I'd taken a lot of leeway at work this month, I could put in the extra time, especially as they've been on my case about not meeting my targets and all! Everything is not about you and how you're feeling. I'm sorry, I didn't explain, but you need to have a little bit more faith..."

And then I fell silent. I felt a little foolish, like I'd just made things worse. "I'm sorry..."

"Thanks," you said. But the smile you gave me didn't quite reach your eyes...

# THIRTY-FOUR

Humility and submission in practice are much harder than one imagines, even if you already know or suspect that it would be difficult... Believe me, you don't know anything yet! It's like trying to cut out a limb, by yourself, using a blunt instrument! *God, this week was hard!*

But it was profitable, that much I'd say. I spent a lot of time crying and praying for God to help me. I learnt about patience, TRUST, surrendering and forsaking... I learnt to doubt myself, put myself in other people's shoes, and also rethink my values...

Because I realised that sometimes, I am not even bothered about things I let myself get bothered about. Sometimes, I act in a way that seems prescribed... I get angry because I think I'm supposed to be. So, now, I'm not easily angered or annoyed by things that you do... I know I still have a long way to go, but I think I'm more understanding and gracious. And I appreciate the efforts you've made too.

I like how you send me messages at work, to let me know how you're doing and to check on me too. I like how you come home with thoughtful gifts like jam, coffee and chocolates... And I especially like how you've been reaching out for me at night, so that now I enjoy nights in your arms, and not just in our bed.

I like how you spoke to me last night, while we laid in bed together, and said you believed in us again. I liked how you apologised again for an issue we'd had and resolved, just because you could see things a little clearer, even though you didn't have to. And most of all, I like, no - I *love* - how you lead our prayer times together these days.

Tonight, we're going bowling. I haven't been in donkey years, and it was back when I was in England. I wonder if you're any good. I've always wanted to go, but you weren't really keen, and there really weren't many options of places to bowl in Lagos, so we never did. I'm really glad that you've decided to take me bowling at last 😁!

The place is not too crowded, but busy enough. We rent our shoes, and the attendant sets up our game, so that we are playing against each other. Now, I understand why we never went bowling. You're completely clueless about the game.

You try your hand on the smaller balls and manage to hit a couple of pins with your first two turns. I enjoy teaching you the little tricks I know or have observed from playing and watching others, and you're a pretty fast learner. As the game progresses, you begin to enjoy it more and take more risks. And what do you know, it's a tie! Yeah, I never said I was good at it. I'm just average.

Now, you're smiling and are eager for another round. However, a young couple approaches us to ask if we would be happy to compete with them. I'm a bit nervous at first, because I'm not that good, and you're new, but I think it would be fun. You're not at all intimidated and seem rather excited by the offer.

It turns out to be a really good game. And I play my best bowling ever! The other couple are pretty average too, so the competition is just right. They are clearly a young couple, and their public displays of affection is quite on the high side, but it's cute...kind of inspiring. I like how you decide to imitate their winner's dance, when they kiss, and give me high fives and loud kisses too, whenever one of us does a strike or double strike.

We end up winning the competition, and it's the perfect end to a fun night. In my excitement, I jump into your arms and you catch me, and kiss me ceremoniously. The other couple, Bose and Marvin, who are actually in their second year of marriage, are laughing at us now.

"Congrats, guys! Good game!" Marvin says, when I'm finally

on my feet again, and feeling very silly.

"Yeah, good game too! Thanks for the invite," you say, holding me close.

"You guys are so inspiring..." Bose says, looking at me emotionally. And then I wonder just what they too must be working through in their marriage.

I look up at you and sigh, as I cuddle in your arms. "Thanks. It was lovely meeting you both."

# THIRTY-FIVE

"So, this is supposed to be our last session. There's still a lot for us to cover, but I think today, it would be good if you both choose what our focus should be, based on your development so far," the counsellor said, looking between us. "And, if you're happy, and you'd like to do the full course, then we can continue with the programme next week..."

I was happy to see you nodding along with me. "Yes, we'd like to continue. I think I can speak for the both of us..." you said.

"Yes, please! Thanks," I said, smiling.

"Great! So, what should our focus be today?"

I looked at you, and it seemed you had something to say, so I waited. "I'd be interested in addressing the issue of finance..."

The counsellor nodded and said, "Yes, that's very important too. Onome, do you have another suggestion?"

"Ummm... Well, I am interested in talking about sex...or intimacy. Like, how we can get it back."

"Hmmm... Good one," the counsellor said.

"Yeah... We can discuss finance next week. I want to talk about sex too," you said, with a small smile.

"Okay... I think intimacy should be the focus then. When you get that right, there should be no problem with talking about sex, even between yourselves. But there's a whole lot more to intimacy than sex. Intimacy is primarily an issue of trust, and we can all see why that would be a challenge right now. You're both dealing with broken trust."

We both nodded.

"You know, trust is very fragile. It is often given in faith, but it is easily shattered, and when it is, it can take a very, very long time to rebuild. You have to be determined to build it up again and to have faith again. To regain trust and intimacy in your marriage, you need to start being honest and sincere with each other. You need to allow yourselves to be vulnerable with each other. You need to actively and intentionally communicate with one another.

"So, no more games. No more lies or half-truths. No more secrets. Also, no more judgement. The condition for complete honesty in a relationship is *unconditional acceptance*. You really need to be extremely gracious with one another, being each other's best friend, so that your spouse can feel safe to tell you *anything*. However, for trust to grow, you mustn't abuse the privilege of forgiveness, grace and acceptance your spouse offers you..."

I nodded, and you sighed.

"In regards to intimacy, you've already taken some big steps to regain it. The first was forgiveness, which we focused on in the first session, then love and romance, then humility and submission... The last door is friendship and trust. You need to learn how to be friends again, then your trust will grow as you choose to interact with each other, communicate honestly, care for each other and *allow yourself* to be looked after by your spouse.

"There are different types of intimacy we need to look at, and they are all very important for getting you back on track for a blissful marriage. One of them is actually *financial* intimacy, which is about having agreement and being honest and transparent with your finances. So, getting intimacy right is fundamental when thinking of working together as a team on building your financial wealth.

"I just want you to know that every day, you're going to have to choose whether to build on trust or to break trust... Every minute of every day. Trust - and intimacy - won't grow if you do not *both* build it *consciously* and *intentionally*. It will wear away and become weak. But by paying attention to the little things you can do to build trust and, ultimately, intimacy, you will grow a strong and happy marriage."

I sighed deeply and you nodded this time. I got a bit emotional, because it was all sounding doable and easy enough, but it's terribly hard. Even with all the progress we have made, I feel like there's still a big gulf between us. I wiped away some tears that seemed to have come from nowhere.

"Thanks for your counsel... I really appreciate the progress we've made, but it's still so hard. We try to talk and listen to one another, and we apologise...but everything's so diplomatic. It doesn't feel spontaneous or natural... Am I expecting too much too soon?"

"Quite possibly, you are. Like I said, trust and intimacy will take time to build again. It's not like forgiveness in the sense that you can just make a decision to forgive. But you have to keep believing and hoping. Through it all, you have to keep praying. Not only for the situation to change, but for *you* to change. And for your hearts to heal from the emotional wounds you've inflicted on one another."

I nodded again. "Thanks... I'll keep praying."

# THIRTY-SIX

It is a true proverb that anyone who wishes to have friends must show himself to be friendly. So is the case for anyone who wants to make friends with their spouse again. We have to be friendly, and that means being kind, pleasant, approachable, attentive, helpful and understanding.

Being friendly is a skill I've had to relearn. Being an introvert, I was never all that friendly to begin with. You had come after me, and well, I'd succumbed after playing hard to get for about a month or so. But now, I couldn't just wait for you to come after me again... I couldn't let you do all the hard work, as if I am some high prize or I have been without fault in our marriage. I also have to make the effort to woo you, my husband, and one of the things I need to learn is how to be friendly...and feminine.

Our month is almost over, and I am pretty confident that we are on a sure path to reconciliation. For our fourth date, we asked my sister to babysit Lara, so that we can enjoy the weekend alone together. It was your idea, and I believe it's just what we need to get reacquainted with ourselves again. But I'm nervous. What are we going to do all weekend?

I wake up early Saturday morning, as is my habit to do, and go to my private place to study and pray. I've been reading through Proverbs all month, and today, I'm reading Proverbs 31, being the last day of the month. I read and draw inspiration from the woman of virtue, who is diligent in business and in her home.

One lesson I take away from today's reading is her faithfulness. I know she didn't get to her level by being discouraged and giving up, because it surely wasn't easy. It was little things she did faithfully that allowed her to grow in esteem in the eyes of her children, husband and the community. With the counselling sessions we've had, I now know what to do; I just need to be diligent, to be faithful to keep doing these little things and trust that the fruit will be borne in time.

"Ummm... Something smells good," you say, as you wrap your arms around me, startling me. I didn't know when you came into the kitchen.

I smile and turn to you, breathing deeply because I feel a little nervous. "Thanks, dear. I'm making pancakes."

You give me a small kiss on my lips, before releasing me. "Cool..." You get yourself a bottle of cold water, before you return to the lounge, while I finish making breakfast.

We have a lovely breakfast at the dining table. I'd cooked sausages and baked beans to go with our pancakes. As we eat, we talk about our plan for the weekend. After breakfast, we would have our baths, then laze about together, watching some shows and/or a movie on television, until the mid-afternoon, when we would take a leisurely walk together around the neighbourhood. Then we'd come home and rest, relax or nap, until the evening, when we'd go out for dinner.

It was a good plan we followed, until we returned home from our afternoon walk. I didn't realise how tired I was, and I chose the option to nap after our walk. You weren't sleepy, so you said you'd do a bit of work, while I rested.

I woke up about 6:30pm, to find you cooking in the kitchen! I swear, you haven't done that more than twice since we've been married. It was such a wonderful sight, even though I was nervous about your hygiene standards! But I decided to trust, and allow myself to be looked after by you...

"Hey, I thought we were supposed to go out for dinner?"

"Yeah... I thought it would be nice to cook for you today," you replied, with a smile. "If it isn't any good, we can order takeaway."

"It'll be good. It smells delish!" I grin. "How can I help?"

"You can set the table...and go and put your feet up."

"Cool..." I said, smiling happily.

At 8pm, dinner is ready and it smells awesome. I serve our plates and you lead in prayer over the meal. Hungrily, I tuck in and swoon with pleasure. The chicken and gizzard you cooked up are so soft and tasty, and the fried rice is on point.

After a few mouthfuls, I can't help but say, "This is delicious! You really should do this more often, Temi."

"Maybe one of these days I'll teach you," you reply and I sigh. I know I need to make more effort in that department. I'm just so used to doing things my own way.

"Sure. I look forward to it," I smile.

# THIRTY-SEVEN

It was really a wonderful day. I was just so at peace throughout. And the best part for me was when we switched off the TV and just talked.

And now you're looking at me in that way that I know you're going to kiss me. And I swallow hard. You reach out your hand and draw my face close to yours before you plant a soft kiss on my lips. I move into your embrace and kiss you back with a burning desire, so strong. And for a while, that's all we're doing...kissing.

Then I feel your hand as it moves my satin dressing gown from my shoulders, exposing my skin to the cool breeze of the air conditioner. With your other hand, you pull at the knot I made with the belt, and it loosens and frees me from the gown, so that you remove it completely from my upper body, revealing my lace bra underneath. I, too, begin to undress you.

You're kissing my neck now, and your tongue is trailing down south. We're doing this, I'm thinking. At last, we're making love again. That's what this is right? This isn't just sex...I hope.

You lean against me, so that I lay back on the sofa, and your hands and lips continue their rounds on my body; caressing, squeezing, stimulating me. And now I'm thinking about protection. I'm no longer on the pill, and I'm not on my period either. If we have sex without protection, there's a good chance I'll conceive. Can I stop you now, when you're so into it...especially when I know you want another child?

"Temi," I mutter between kisses. You look into my eyes and they're glazed over.

"Onome, I've missed you," you say, passionately. You remove the last of your underwear and we're both naked. If I don't say something now, it'll be too late. But if I do, you might lose interest...

"Temi..." I mutter again, and you groan into my neck.

You raise yourself up and look into my eyes, and I know we're thinking the same thing. And I know you want to proceed, and you want me to surrender to the moment. You want me to give in to you and trust you and let love happen.

I swallow. There's the other issue of STDs that I don't want to think about. *God, why am I being so negative when what I've desired is finally happening?*

"Onome, are you okay?" you ask, beginning to pull away, but I hold you close.

"I love you, Temi," I say those words I haven't said in years to you, because I thought I didn't mean them. Now, I know I do. I love you, and that's all that matters to me. And that's my surrender.

You take it and kiss me fiercely. Moments later, you're in me and we're one again, moving in rhythm and pleasure. You're making love to me, and it's so deep. It's more than physical. I feel a release of my soul, from chains of fear, pride and guilt. I feel like a woman released of her demons as I come in your arms. *I love you.*

***

The next morning, I wake up in your arms, feeling unbelievably free and happy. We made love twice last night, and it was amazing. It was cleansing, like a new beginning.

It is a new week, a new month, a new quarter. The Sunday morning sun shines brilliantly into our bedroom and a refreshing breeze blows through, enveloping us with love. I take in a deep breath and release it with a smile, as I open my eyes. It is both a shock and a pleasure to see you staring down at me. By the looks of things, you've been awake for a while, watching me.

"Good morning, darling," you say, before you lean in to give me a soft kiss on my lips.

Is this the better? I hope this is the beginning of the better, because I've had enough of the worse. I swallow, looking into your eyes, begging the question. *Temi, I never dreamt we'd get here... And now I'm thinking it was worth the fight, but I hope we never go back there.*

"Good morning, hubby," I smile up at you, and you pull me in for a hug.

In the distance, I can see a tray with a jug and condiments for tea, and I can smell the eggs and sausages, which are hidden inside small coolers. *You made breakfast!* However, the way you are looking at me now, and the slow determination of your hands on my body tells me that breakfast is going to have to wait. *Oh, Lord, bind us together forever*, I pray in my spirit, as I give myself to you again.

# VOLUME SEVEN

*"If any of you lack wisdom, let him ask of God, that giveth to all men liberally, and upbraideth not; and it shall be given him. But let him ask in faith, nothing wavering. For he that wavereth is like a wave of the sea driven with the wind and tossed..."*
(James 1:5-6).

## THIRTY-EIGHT

Oh Lord, what is happening to me? Why am I feeling this way...? We've been here before, and done this before... How do I know that this time is for real?

I love Mirabel... At least I thought I did. I do. I know I do. She's incredible. She's sweet and thoughtful. But she's not Onome.

I'm still married to Onome, and now that we've made love - twice - I know she won't want to sign the papers. I don't even know if I still want her to. God, I'm so confused!

I really didn't think this counselling thing would change anything. There was a part of me that was curious to see if it could, which was why I gave it my all...sure that it would not. And now look at where we are, and what I've done!

Why did I sleep with Onome? And why do I feel this dread like a defendant awaiting the pronouncement of his judgement to life imprisonment...but also feel like a juvenile delinquent being given a second chance to stay home and prove himself? I feel both happy and sad, because I have to choose. I can't remain juvenile and delinquent, if I want to stay home, but again I feel like what I'm giving up, my liberty to come and go as I please, is too high a cost to pay for peace.

My phone vibrates on the bedside table on my side of the bed, and I quickly pick it up before Onome wakes up. It's Mirabel. Why's she calling me so early? It must be important.

I quietly creep out of bed and go to the living room to answer the call. My heart is beating fast, because I'm nervous that Onome might wake up soon and find me crouched in the dark, whispering on the phone to my girlfriend, the morning after we reconciled. I better make this a quick call.

"Hey, ba...Mirabel. What's up?" Somehow, calling her "babe" now, when I'm not even sure what's going to happen between us feels so wrong.

"Temi... I need to see you." Already, I can tell she's been crying. I feel sad and I want to go to her and hug her and tell her everything will be fine.

"What's the matter, babe?" I couldn't help it. She's still my babe...right now.

"I can't talk over the phone. Can I see you this morning? Or maybe for lunch?"

I shake my head, and then as though realising that she can't see me, say, "I'm sorry, babe. Can't do today. Let's see tomorrow."

Mirabel sniffles. "It's been a month, Temi. You said you needed a month. Is this how it's going to be now? Will she always come first?! Or have you changed your mind about us?"

Wow! I didn't see that coming. Suddenly, I feel a headache coming on. The pressure is too much. I don't even know what to say.

"Mirabel... This is hard for me," I say. I lower my voice as I add, "I love you...but there's so much more to marriage."

"Is she there?" Mirabel asks suddenly. Not waiting for my response, she adds, "Did you sleep with her?"

My silence speaks volumes. "Oh, God!" I hear her cry into the phone. "You slept with her!"

I can't take this anymore. I have to get off the phone. I need to pray. I need some direction. I need a word from You, Lord.

"Babe, I have to go," I say, as I hang up the phone. And then I cry like I haven't cried in years.

"Oh, God, I'm sorry! I've made such a mess of everything! I

don't know what to do. I don't know how to feel... And I can't even trust my feelings. One day, I want to make things work with Onome. And the next, I wonder if this is just another phase...and then we will get back to reality, where we are both miserable.

"I know I still love her. I felt it last night. I remembered how things had been in the beginning...how much I wanted her before we got married, and even the way I felt that night I proposed to her. Yes, things have changed, but she's still the Onome I wanted to spend the rest of my life with. I just never thought it would get this hard!

"Lord, I'm torn between these two women. I can't choose...but I don't want to lose them both. Please help me! Please make Your will clear to me. If You will just show me the way, and promise to go with me every step, I will be faithful. I'm so tired of feeling like a fool!"

I fall to my knees, where I continue to weep. And I wait on You to speak to me. A word of truth and liberation. Of power and love. And then I hear You, clear in my spirit: "*What the Lord has joined together, let not man separate.*"

# THIRTY-NINE

Eventually, I rise up and decide to make breakfast for my wife. It's my repentance meal. It's my declaration of commitment to us. I know that You have brought us back together again, and I know that if You are with us, nothing can come between us. Not even my love for Mirabel.

I'll have to tell her that it's over. That I'm choosing Onome, my wife. That I choose You.

As I make the breakfast, joy enters my heart. I know I am doing the right thing. I am walking in Your will, in the way of miracles. It's already a wonder to me how Onome and I could get back here, knowing how badly we both fell. And my resolve is strengthened. We are going to work. Our love is going to grow and last forever.

I'm smiling as I carry the tray to our bedroom. I'm happy to see that she's still sleeping. She looks so peaceful and happy, and beautiful. I go to draw the curtains and open the window for some cool fresh breeze.

I climb back into bed, and lean over her, just as the clouds shift and the sun's intense rays pour into our room. It seems like a divine blessing. And the wind that sweeps through the room, stirring my wife from her sleep, confirms Your presence in this home, in this marriage. I breathe in deeply, happy. Everything's going to be alright.

***

We lie in bed, spent after making love. It was spontaneous and yet so deliberate, like a spiritual cleansing. She's resting her head on my chest now, while my heart thumps in its cage. I never knew I could feel this way again...for this woman.

"Do you want to go to Church today?" she suddenly asks, turning to look at me and sitting up in bed.

I wonder about the time, positive we had already missed the last service, and turn to retrieve my phone from the bedside table. It's not there. I guess I left it in the living room.

Honestly, I don't feel like going to Church this morning. This, *this* connection and reconciliation is so much more important and powerful, and I think THIS is Church. And I remember Your word that where two or three are together in Your name, You are there with them. I smile and feel relieved.

"Not today, dear. Let's bond some more. I'm loving this. I feel God's presence here...with just us two."

Onome breathes in deeply. "Yeah, me too. I guess I was thinking it would be good if we could do thanksgiving for all God has done. We've been through a lot, and I'm burning to sing His praises for seeing us through."

I smile and pull her in for a hug. "I feel you. We can go for the evening service. I just feel like spending the day in bed with you."

She nods and lifts her head up to kiss me briefly, before excusing herself to go to the bathroom. When she returns, we have a prayer time and then enjoy breakfast in bed. Then we talk some more.

*** 

Oh Lord, You are so amazing! Onome told me what You did for her. How You delivered her again from condemnation... How You revealed Yourself to her in a whole new way. And how You sent her back to me, to deliver me from a pit of sin, despair and condemnation.

I can't but fall on my face and worship You now...

"God, who is there like You?! There is no one so awesome! Your mercy astounds me. Your grace empowers me. Your love sets me free...

"I am not worthy of Your love nor grace. I spat in Your face and shunned You. I said I loved You, but I lied. When it was time to live it, I denied You...I forsook my cross. Lord, if not for Your mercy and faithfulness, where would I be?

"God, I know that the devil will never relent from tempting us. So, please help us to be strong. Help us to be faithful and true. Deliver us from all his devices, to the glory of Your name alone, amen!"

# FORTY

What an amazing weekend! After our rest and fellowship in the morning, we decided to go out for lunch. It was a late one, and we were both relaxed and happy. And for once, I wasn't trying to be. And I could tell she was genuine too.

We'd connected deeply in the morning, after she'd told me about her heavenly experience. I had that moment of "if God is for me, who can be against me?", seeing how peaceful she was. Like, who was I to hold her sins against her when You had pardoned her and washed her clean and commissioned her to go forth and minister to others? Who was I to say she's not able, when You believe in her? And through her, I heard You clearly say You believe in us...and You believe in me. Thank You for this grace.

I'm at work now and I'm still in awe of You. I feel like there's a fountain of life bubbling within me. I feel so much joy I can barely contain it. And so, I'm singing worship songs, softly under my breath, and getting strange looks from my co-workers in nearby cubicles.

Several of them know by now that I have been having marital issues. Not only have they seen me with Mirabel, I've told them about her, and grumbled about Onome severally. And now I feel ashamed. I'm sure they are wondering why on Earth I will be singing gospel music, when my Christianity seems non-existent.

I spoiled my witness, I know that now. But I have You to

thank that it's not over yet! And Your word washes me clean again, as I recall the scripture: "*For a righteous man may fall seven times and rise again, but the wicked shall fall by calamity*" (Proverbs 24:16). I smile and sing a little louder, the gospel track by Newsboys; "Amazing Love (You Are My King)".

At 12pm, I get a text message from Mirabel asking if we're still meeting for lunch. I can't believe I've forgotten about her. Yes, she called a few times yesterday, but I couldn't pick nor return her calls. Plus, we were at our Fellowship at the time. I'd already told her we couldn't meet yesterday and needed some time to think things through. But I'd intended to contact her this morning. I don't want to string her along.

So, I reply back to confirm time with her. We have a usual spot on Ajose where we used to have lunch, because our offices are on the same street. After I send the message, I get a message from Chudi. He seems to be so in the Spirit, so I decide to read his message right away, hoping it's a timely word.

"*Hey Temi, how's your day going? I thought to get in touch and remind you how much God loves you. Nothing you do or have done will ever change that, but we live our best lives when we embrace His love and let Him take control! Abide in Him and have a great day, Brother.*"

And timely it was. I reply back: "*Thanks bro! It's going good. God loves you too.*"

***

It's ten minutes past our lunch time, and Mirabel hasn't come in yet. I send Onome a message while I'm waiting, to let her know I'm thinking of her. She hasn't seen it yet, so I just chill and browse Instagram while I wait.

There's a new post from Mirabel. As usual, she's posted a recent picture of herself and an encouraging message for women. I usually don't read them, because...well, I'm a guy... But today, I'm a little curious. As I click to read, the thought occurs to me that I should unfollow her on social media, but I think it's a little harsh, so I dismiss it.

"*Ladies, don't settle for less. Know what you want and be ready to make the sacrifices to get it. Don't expect that life will place everything in your path or think that if you have to struggle it's not meant to be. Love is a battlefield. You get what you fight or settle for! Much love xoxo*"

*Hmmm... That's not encouraging*, I'm thinking. It's darn right scary!

As I'm musing on the post, I feel a shadow over me. Someone has blocked out the light. I look up to find Mirabel standing across from me, and my heart races. It's been so long since we've seen each other, and I almost forgot what a slay queen she is. Yet, the way she's just standing there, watching me and hovering over me is a little creepy.

I rise up to hug her, and she's a little tense. After we sit, I can tell something's wrong. She's upset about something...

"You alright?" I ask, wondering if she's going to save me the trouble and break up with me herself. But no such luck.

"I'm pregnant."

# FORTY-ONE

"You're what?"

"I said I'm pregnant," she says a little louder. And we both look around, wondering who's listening and who heard. I swallow hard, sit up straight and take in some deep breaths.

"Are you sure?" To that, she rolls her eyes. "But we used protection."

"It's not 100%, you know! Look, I just thought you should know."

I'm nodding and thinking...*God why???* But I know I only have myself to blame. Still, *God why???!!!* I thought You were going to make this easy for me?! This will change everything! *It doesn't have to*, I hear You say in my spirit, and remember Chudi's message about abiding in Jesus no matter what.

"So...have you made up your mind?" I'm looking at her blankly, trying to regain focus, because there's like a wave of confusion about to drown me. "About us?" She has a hint of a smile on her face, and I can see she's insecure; unsure but hopeful. Of course, she thinks this will favour her! *Wait, is it genuine?*

I scratch my head, unsure how to ask the question. "How...how do you know? Did you see a doctor?"

She sighs deeply. "I took a home test. I know, alright? My period is also late, and it's never late."

"Hmm hmmm," I nod, and run my hand through my head. "Wow..." The thought occurs to me to ask if she's going to keep it, but I interrupt it with *of course*! I wouldn't encourage her to abort a baby, especially my baby. And I'm a little excited wondering if it's going to be a boy. *God, what is this madness?!* I seriously don't know how to feel, not to mention deal, with this situation. Then I remember that it's not just about me. "Are you okay?"

Mirabel smiles, and I realise that she's been waiting for me to ask her that. And I feel a bit better, like I passed the test. I'm not a terrible person. "I'm fine," she says. "Been a little nauseous, but I'm happy...if you are..."

Is this another test? *God, give me grace!* "Ummm... That's good. Does anyone else know?" She shakes her head. "Do you know how far gone you are?"

She shrugs. "A month or two. I'll know when I see the doctor. I hope you're not thinking I should abort it!"

"Of course, not!" I say. Perhaps a bit too emphatic, as she blossoms with a wide smile, almost as if I said "*I love you.*"

"Oh, good." She stretches out her hand to hold mine on the table. "Temi, I know this is hard for you... And I forgive you for yesterday... But, I think this is just what we need to see that what we have is beautiful and worth fighting for."

Alarm bells are ringing in my head and in my heart and in my spirit. This seems so wrong. I feel like screaming. How am I going to tell Onome about this? How will she react? Clearly, Mirabel thinks this saves us... But does it? *NO!* The word is clear in my spirit. I'm not going to let this take me back, and out of the will of God.

I squeeze her hand as I look into her eyes and say as sincerely as I can, "Mirabel... I've done a lot of thinking and praying, and even though I haven't really factored this new information into it, I've decided that I'm going to work things out with my wife... I'm sorry for..."

She pulls her hand away. "No, Temi. You can't do this to me... To us! I won't let you!"

Now, I know we have an audience. She's going to make a scene, and I'm just thinking how did I not see this coming? "*Sssshhh...*" I attempt to quieten her down. But anyone who knows women knows that's the worst thing you can do at such a time!

"Don't *shush* me! Don't *ever*!" And I'm just staring at her, willing her to calm down, and threatening with my eyes to leave if she doesn't, because God knows that's all I can do now. She gets the message and reduces her volume, but it's too little too late. Our audience is already tuned in, even though many are pretending not to be listening or watching the unfolding drama. "Temi, I love you... And I know you love me. So, I'm going to give you more time to think about this, and make the right decision..."

And to my surprise and relief, she stands up and leaves me sitting there; ashamed, embarrassed, disgraced...but forgiven.

# FORTY-TWO

I still haven't told Onome about the baby. I've been waiting for the right time and trying to think of the best way to bring it up, but, as each day passes, I'm realising that the right time has come and gone severally...and there is no right way to tell her. I'm going to have to just tell her and face the music.

It's Wednesday and we're at our fifth counselling session, and I feel like a phoney. Onome is so happy and thinks that we're on the right track and on the same page. However, the more I've pondered on Mirabel's pregnancy, the more unsure and confused I have become about my decision to abide in my marriage, even though things are getting better between us... Marriage counselling didn't prepare us for this, and all of a sudden, I want to know, what would the counsellor say to this? What is the quick fix solution that I can't see?

"Mirabel's pregnant," I suddenly blurt out.

The counsellor, who was just talking, stops mid-speech and Onome turns to look at me, alarmed. This wasn't how I wanted her to find out, but at least we have a mediator in case things get out of hand. I just needed to get it out of my head and out there, where it's not such a big mountain anymore, but just another problem that can be solved.

"Okay..." the counsellor speaks first. Onome has covered her face with her hands and I can see she's getting emotional. I don't know how to comfort her. "Do you want to talk about that?"

I nod, afraid to speak, because I can't trust my tongue not to betray me.

"How do you feel about that?" the counsellor asks.

"Disappointed," I manage to say after a while.

"In what exactly?"

"In myself..." I swallow. *Excited too. Admit it. There's a little excitement there too.* "And a little excited...if I'm honest," *Oh, God! I shouldn't have said that.*

Onome gasps and looks at me. It's like she wants to say something, but she doesn't. She keeps her eyes on the counsellor.

"*Excited?* What are you excited about?" the counsellor continues her questioning.

I try to shrug it off. "I mean...having a baby. It's a good thing, isn't it? I mean, I know it's bad that it's not Onome's, but it's still a blessing..." *Word vomit! Okay, stop talking.* "I want more children...and hopefully a boy." *Okay, you've really messed up now. Don't you know when to keep your mouth shut?!*

"Hmmm... Onome, you've been quiet..." the counsellor says, looking at Onome and sliding her a box of tissues.

She takes one, dabs her eyes and sniffles. "There's nothing to say..."

"So, what do you want to do about Mirabel's pregnancy, Temi?"

"I don't know... I don't know... I thought saying something might help... But I guess not." I look at Onome, and then back at the counsellor, as I say, "She doesn't want to let me go..."

Onome huffs and laughs mockingly. "She doesn't want to let you go??? *Please!* You don't want to let her go! She comes back to you *claiming* to have your child and you're ready to throw everything away for *her*! Have you forgotten that you already have a child and a family...? Have you forgotten everything we've learnt this past month...or did nothing get through to you at all?!"

"Onome, calm down," the counsellor says. But I wish she wouldn't. I want to hear everything she has to say...and I'm praying it will help me decide and stick to my decision.

"You know what? This is what *you* want! This is the out you've been waiting for. Here I was, thinking you're in control and you're going to make a decision and fight for us, where as I am the one you're hoping will give up and let you go...so you can do whatever you want!"

*Wow! How does she know?* I'm staring at her, waiting for the last ball to drop...wondering if my survival instinct will kick in and change this outcome at the last minute. But like the defendant on trial I watch her, not sure which way she will go, but making my peace with her decision.

"You know what? I deserve better."

And to my surprise, she rises up and leaves the room. I just sit there with my head in my hands, unable to move to go after her and unable to think. I just want to scream. *Why is this so hard???!!*

# FORTY-THREE

I know, I messed up. I was so sure, until I was not. I remembered how unhappy I used to be, and how happy I had been with Mirabel...and I thought only of me. It is certain that if ever I stop feeling happy with Mirabel, I will think only of me and walk out. If marriage and parenthood can't make me a man of integrity and responsibility, what hope is there for me in an ordinary relationship...a carnal relationship, where my desires and will dictate my actions?

God, I'm a mess! And it's because of this fact that I can't run after Onome. I can't assure her of my faithfulness and love. I can't offer her security from my whimsicalness. Tomorrow, I might change my mind. Unfortunately, that's who I am right now - a double-minded man. But God, You are still God! *So, please help me!!!*

There was nothing more to say after Onome walked out of the counselling room. I left for the office a minute or two after and I'm only just returning home, at about 10pm. I didn't hurry back because I had much to do at the office, and I also needed space to think through a lot of things.

I go to our bedroom, after checking the kitchen and confirming that there is nothing prepared for dinner. Onome must still be angry with me, but I'm still not ready to talk about it, because I haven't settled on what I want to do yet. The lamp by my side of the bed is still on, and it's shining brightly on a document on the table. My heart thumps in my chest. *Is that what I think it is?*

I swallow as I draw closer and pick up the papers. It's our divorce papers. The second one I drew up. I turn quickly to the last page and surely, it's signed. Onome has signed the divorce papers...?! *Because Mirabel is pregnant?*

*No. Because that's what you wanted.* And that's when the truth hits me. This is not about the baby.

***

It's been a week, and I'm back at the counselor's office...alone. I desperately need someone to talk to, because I'm still confused. I haven't really been able to pray, and I don't know why. Everything just feels at a standstill, and every way I imagine taking seems like a dead end.

I haven't told anyone about the divorce papers, not even Mirabel. They're still in my bag, and I haven't filed them yet. I am waiting for clarity, for certainty. I'm just waiting.

"How are you today, Temi?" she asks, with a small smile on her face. I know, I didn't think I'd be caught dead in a therapist's office that I wasn't dragged into.

I cough and try to smile. "I'm okay. Actually, I'm not... But, yeah..."

She nods. "I think I understand. How's Onome?"

"I don't know... She divorced me."

"Hmmm... I thought it was you who drafted the papers..."

"Well, she signed them. We were reconciling. I didn't think she would."

"Okay... Have you filed them?"

"Not yet."

"Okay, so what do you want from me? From this?"

I let out a deep breath. "I need counsel. I need...help."

"Okay... And, ummm... How is Mirabel?"

"She's fine. She did her first scan yesterday."

"Did you go with her?"

"No... She didn't tell me about it before hand. She sent the picture by WhatsApp."

"Ummm... So, how do you feel about that?"

"It's strange. The picture wasn't clear. Would have loved to have known about the scan beforehand."

"Oh, okay. I meant how you feel about being a father again... I guess you'd like to be more involved...?"

"Yeah... Yeah. I'm also nervous about how our relationship will change...is already changing."

"What do you mean?"

"Ummm... Well, all she talks about now is the baby...and our future. It's a bit much, all of a sudden."

The counselor nods as she jots something down in her pad. "Ummm... Do you think you might have a problem with commitment?"

I look up at her and we lock eyes for a second. I know what she's thinking. That I don't really want what I think I want because I'm not mature enough to handle what I truly want. And she's right. I have some - a lot of - growing up to do.

# VOLUME EIGHT

*"There is no fear in love; but perfect love casteth out fear: because fear hath torment. He that feareth is not made perfect in love"*
(1 John 4:18).

## FORTY-FOUR

I should have seen it coming.

*Why didn't I see this coming?* I was so sure that God was on our side and was working all things out for our good, that I didn't prepare my mind nor heart for this. I know He's always in control, so I can't but wonder why He would let this happen?! I really wish I could see His whole plan...

I wanted to let it go, like I know I'm supposed to. Forgive him. Especially as the pregnancy is merely a consequence and not the sin. I wanted to believe that we would get past it, but it was just clear to me that Temi didn't feel the same way. It was clear that he didn't want me. He was being dragged along for the ride and was not man enough to make a decision!

As I looked back over the last week, remembering the night I gave myself to him again and told him I loved him, I remembered so clearly how he'd said nothing. But I didn't want to make an issue out of it. I wasn't going to force him to say he loved me. Besides, men tend to say it with their actions more than words.

I guess that's why it hurt so much. His silence and the way he brought up the issue about his pregnant girlfriend, in the middle of our marriage counseling session, and was still waiting for someone to tell him what to do, was the sign I heeded. I was in the marriage alone, and would continue to be, as long as he let me decide for him.

So, as hard as it was, I had to set him free. I can't spend my whole life wondering if or when he'll leave me because I forced him to stay, when he wanted to go... I gave it my best shot. I gave it faith and love. And now, all there is is hope.

Hope that he will do what is right in the end... But regardless, I'm going to live. Marriage isn't the be all and end all of my existence. I know that regardless of my failure, and whatever my marital status, God is still God and I am still a child, grafted in by His grace and that alone. I am just going to keep following Him, trusting Him and obeying Him.

Still, it wasn't easy coming to that decision; to sign the divorce papers. I laboured in my spirit for hours, trying to discern God's voice and silence mine. I was definitely angry and frustrated. God had called me to surrender, and I was ready to accommodate the child, knowing how tough it would be. Knowing that this woman might continue to be a thorn in my marriage.

However, the scripture is clear that "*a double-minded man is unstable in all his ways...*" And so, I decided to let go and let God. I realised that Temi needs to figure out what he wants and what God's will is; with or without me.

In my mind, we're separated, and I am going to use this time to draw nearer to God and grow into His will for me. I'll also keep praying for Temi. My primary prayer point is for his soul to find peace and joy in God, and not for him to come back to me so that our marriage will "work". Together or apart, we can glorify God. I know that now.

For myself, I just pray that God will keep my eye single towards Him. That He will remain the source of my joy and my refuge at all times. I'm not looking for a knight in shining armour anymore. I'm no longer looking to Temi or any man to validate me as a woman or as a person. In Him I move and have my being. That's the truth I want to experience and live every day from now on.

So, today would have been our sixth counseling session. I'm no longer angry, and I'm not even sad. I am...free. That's the best word that describes how I am feeling right now. I am also hopeful and joyful.

I decided to go to the office today. I got the job I applied for at

JV Media and went in to meet with my boss at JV Magz to discuss how I could do both. As much I appreciate the promotion to be an Editor for the magazine, it's been my dream to write stories for TV and movies. She said she was confident I could do both, and that she wasn't at all anxious about my competence. It was quite a relief, and a boost of my confidence. I start next month and I'm pretty excited about it.

So, I'm thankful. And optimistic... The future is bright ☺.

# FORTY-FIVE

It's August, and I'm starting my new job as a script writer with JV Media. Lara is home for the summer holidays now, so daycare is a bit of a challenge. I'm still not comfortable leaving her at home with the house help for hours. It was much easier when I worked freelance, even though it was still hard to write whenever she was home, but at least then, I managed my own time, and didn't have regular meetings to contend with.

Fortunately, I found a day centre near the office in Victoria Island, which closes at 3pm. I had to get special permission to leave early, and have our meetings earlier, so that I could pick her up. It's stressful joggling everything, but I'm managing. But most of all, I'm happy. I'm doing everything I love.

I am working with a team of screen play developers on a new series for TV. They work long hours each day to make sure they meet all the deadlines for the production, from script to a fully edited programme, with scheduled adverts. In the team there is a Programme/Content Director, Associate Producer, Production Manager, Lead Script Writer, me and two other Script Writers. One of them is a Consultant Script Writer from the company sponsoring the programme, whose agenda is to make sure the script is well branded to promote their business, I'm told. We're still at the brainstorming stage, though. By the end of the week, we should have come up with the script for the pilot and first two episodes, so that we can stay ahead of the production team. It's all so exciting!

"Have we settled on a name yet?" I chip in, after introductions have been made, and a briefing on the type of story we're writing and why, has been given by the Production Manager, Anita.

"Yes, we have three ideas so far, but haven't settled on one yet. Once we get the story line going, we should be able to fix that too," Obi, the Lead Script Writer says.

"Cool..." I reply and proceed to listen. I have a lot to learn and little to contribute at this stage. I also don't want to get shut down too early, because of over-eager and not well-thought-out ideas.

"I was thinking we could open with a very dramatic scene, like a fire or something. And then the pilot episode will look at what led to that fire... We can go back like 24 hours before the fire," Bayo, one of the script writers said.

"I think that could work..." Sule, the Associate Producer nods in agreement.

"Yeah, the fire is a good idea. We can include a scene where people are on their phones recording the event for YouTube or Instagram, and get a close up of one of them posting on one of our smart devices," Nathan, the consultant from NGNow Mobile chips in. I try not to laugh, and see Obi's fighting the same urge. Mobile service providers are so typical when it comes to promoting their brands.

"Any other ideas," Obi asks. He's looking at me, as if waiting on my contribution.

I swallow. I'm not sure I'm ready yet. "I like the retrospective idea and dramatic beginning. But maybe we can write about something more common and close to people's hearts, like infidelity. We can still start from the dramatic scene where the cheater gets caught...and then look back 24 hours before," I say at last, with a shrug, wondering if my idea isn't too typical.

"I love it," Onyeka, the Programme Director says. "The best stories are close to home. Good one, Onome."

And the room of writers nod their approval. I can't believe I wasn't shut down. I must be blushing red with embarrassment. "Thanks," was all I could say.

"Yeah... It's a good idea. But let's not do the typical man cheater story. I think it should be the woman whom the man walks in on. There'll definitely be an interesting story behind why she's cheating," Obi says, his eyes narrowing as he looks at me, and then about the room for agreement.

I'm just trying to think whether or not I said it was a male cheater. I'm pretty sure I left it open. But it's a good point, nonetheless, so I nod along with everyone else. I can see he takes his lead role seriously and competitively. I square my shoulders, with a resolve to make my contributions heard.

"So, Scene One..." Onyeka shoots off.

# FORTY-SIX

Before I knew it, I'd spent a month at JV Media. We've completed enough episodes of "Fire On The Mountain" for one quarter, but we are still scripting the series. The production team is already working on casting so that we can start shooting the show this month, to start airing weekly from October, for the last quarter.

We decided to keep the fire scene, which was caused by the scented candles the cheating housewife had used to make her love scene. The husband actually didn't come home to find his wife cheating, but by the end of Season One, when the investigations into the cause of the fire and other related events concludes, he would be in the know...just like all his neighbours, who had been suspecting his wife of foul play. *Ghen ghen!*

It is so different writing a story with other writers chipping in. I think it is better but more challenging...and slow! Left to me, I'd already be writing Season Two! I am also interested in getting some spiritual lessons out of the story, instead of it just being entertaining, so I've often had to wrestle to get my ideas incorporated into the storyline. I like how the story is progressing so far, though, and I can't wait until they start airing it.

Anyway, now that Lara has resumed school, I have to wake up an hour earlier than usual to drop her off at 7:30, before navigating my way through traffic to the office in Victoria Island. She's in Primary One now. I can't believe it... How time flies. I still remember when I was pregnant with her. It was the most stress-free pregnancy, and she remained a low-stress baby. Thank God!

I smile, as I touch my tummy. There's another one in there. I found out a couple of weeks ago, but I'm not showing yet. Still a few weeks before it becomes obvious.

I really wish no one will find out until the last minute, because I really don't want it to affect my work. I just got this job! I'm hoping we'd have finished with scripting Season One before I have to make any announcement, and I can be back in full swing, when they're ready to script Season Two.

I haven't told Temi either. I honestly don't know how to tell him. Since he moved out in July, we have reverted back to not speaking. I keep wondering when I'm going to get the letter in the mail saying that our divorce is final. Maybe then, I'll tell him. I just don't want it to factor into his decision making...since he chose his girlfriend's baby over our family. The last thing I want is for him to come back because of a child. And what if it's another girl? So, I'm just staying low-key with this.

"A penny for your thoughts..."

I look up to see the charming Obinna Okafor at my desk, looking down at me with amusement. I straighten up quickly, trying to remember what I'm supposed to be doing. I smile up at him, a little spacey. Pregnancy seems to make me forgetful.

"Hi, Obi," I say, eventually.

He pulls up a seat and sits with his chest against the back rest, looking at me. "Are you okay?"

I nod, wondering what he might have noticed. "Yeah... I'm fine. What's up?"

He shrugs. "I don't know. I'm just a little curious about you. You're so vocal in the meetings, and then you just sit quietly minding your own business the rest of the time. It's pretty relaxed here, y'know. You should come out for lunch once in a while."

"Thanks for the offer. I'm really trying to manage my funds by not eating out."

"It's okay. You can bring your own. Most people do. It's just cool to hang together at the cafeteria."

"Oh, okay. Thanks," I swallow. I feel a little strange because it seems he has more to say. Obi, Mr Confident, is never lost for words. You can usually find him at other writers' desks chatting away and laughing, so him coming over isn't so strange. It's his awkwardness.

"Well, I can see you're not married," he says suddenly, his eyes skimming from my now bare fingers to my face. "Are you seeing someone?"

Now I understand his discomfort. I knew I saw him giving me a side eye the other day he was at Bayo's desk and they were laughing about God knows what. I shake my head. And he smiles.

"Oh, but no", I add quickly. "I'm not available to date. I just want to be alone for now."

"Oh," he says, sounding a little hurt. "Getting over someone?"

"Not so much. Just trying to enjoy me," I say, with a smile, which I hope he will understand the meaning of.

He nods and rises from his seat. "Aight... Well, see you later, Onome."

I let out a sigh after he's gone. It's nice to be sought after again. But I'm so far from where he is. I don't know if I'll ever want a man again. There's got to be more to life...

# FORTY-SEVEN

So, one day, after we were dismissed from a production meeting, I returned to my desk, accompanied by Anita, who'd taken me under her wing to show me the ropes since I joined the team. Even though she is three years older, we'd gotten so close in such a short time, and I found that I could talk to her about any and everything. She is the only one who knows about my still pending divorce and the full story behind that. Anyway, something strange happened that day...

"Eh heh... You didn't tell me today's your birthday," Anita said, as we approached my desk. I thought that was a weird statement until I followed her gaze to see some flowers on my desk.

"Birthday?! No, oh..." I said, as I hastened to pick up the card that sat on top of the flowers, waiting to be picked by any nosy busybody. Who would have sent these? My first thought went to Obi, wondering if he'd failed to get the message that I am unavailable. But he hadn't acted untoward since.

"What does it say?" Anita asked, picking up the bouquet of mixed flowers and sniffing them.

"With love from a secret admirer... *Secret admirer?*" I rolled my eyes and hissed. An unusual action for a former hopeless romantic. But now, I'm so sick of the idea of love and romance. I just want to be left alone to regain my sanity. I really had no time for such childish games. When we're not in secondary school!

"You have a secret admirer?! You this babe!" Anita chuckled.

"I wonder if it's someone in the office..."

I didn't want to tell her my suspicions, because I had to confirm first. But before I could, I saw him walk by my desk and give me a strange look. It wasn't the look of a secret admirer. It was the look of a jealous admirer wondering about his competition. *So, it wasn't Obi?* I swallowed and put the card away. Now, I was actually curious.

I couldn't help the warm feeling that began to rise in me at the realisation that I had another fan. Someone thought I was wonderful. And for now, it didn't matter who it was. I happily took the compliment and smiled.

"Hmmm... Na wa oh... But he never try now... Where are the chocolates?!" Anita objected and all I could do was laugh.

\*\*\*

The following week, I received more flowers and this time they came with chocolates. That fact alone made me look about the office suspiciously. Had the person overheard our conversation last week? Why couldn't they just come out of hiding already? Not that I was interested or anything. Just to end the suspense.

"I'm sure it's someone in the office," Anita said, as she put a piece of Galaxy chocolate in her mouth and swooned. "Oh, God, these are delicious!"

"And my favourite... Does that mean my admirer is a stalker?!" I asked jokingly, but actually a little creeped out. No one here knew me so well as to know my favourite chocolate brand. But I suppose it could be a lucky guess.

"Hmmm... That's a point... If I were you, I'd be careful, though I think everyone's pretty harmless here. Just be careful sha."

And like clockwork, the next week, I took delivery of more flowers, and this time, they came with cupcakes. My admirer had more to say in his card today. *"I'm ready to love you forever..."*

"Isn't that from Tevin Campbell's song?" Anita asked, taking the card to look at the wording. "This hand-writing..." she mused, obviously feeling like one detective.

Though I was loving the attention (I mean, who doesn't like being fancied?), I wasn't loving the game. I wished whoever it was would come right out and announce themselves, so I could tell them it wasn't happening. I didn't need this type of attention nor distraction... I just want peace of mind and heart.

I decided to ask the security guard to turn away more deliveries. I wrote a short note for him to give to whoever was delivering these flowers, saying "*Thanks but not interested*", and asked him to pass it on when next they came. But it didn't work!

"What happened?!" I'd gone downstairs, frustrated, to inquire into why he hadn't delivered my message. The silly man had smiled sheepishly, saying the Oga had given him N2,000 to deliver the package.

"Sorry, ma!" he shouted after me, as I stormed back upstairs, irritated. I didn't have money to be bribing security so that he could refuse money from a determined pest!

When I got back up to my office, I rather threw the flowers in the bin along with the chocolates, as my sign of protest. If the joker was in the office, he'd surely get the message. However, when I received a card the following day from this so-called admirer slash stalker, my blood practically ran cold as I read it.

"*I know your secret... Let's talk. Meet me at the Bar across the street after work. I'll come to your table. Love, your secret admirer.*"

*What secret?!* I stared at the card and then looked about the room slowly. Who was this person, and what did they want from me?!

# FORTY-EIGHT

Thinking that perhaps I'd misread his expression the first week, I decided to confront Obi, to find out if he was the one sending me the flowers and confusing notes. He had to know it was neither romantic nor funny, especially when he's now talking about knowing my secret! *Like, who does that?!*

At lunchtime, I met him at the Cafeteria. I actually hadn't taken his offer to go there since our conversation that other day. I liked to have my lunch in front of my laptop, as I wrote or browsed the Internet. I was not one for chit chat.

"Obi, do you have a minute?" I asked, when I got to his table. He was with a couple of the guys from the audio-visual team, and I gave a small smile in greeting to them.

"Sure," he said, as he rose up.

"Are you the one sending me the flowers?!" I asked immediately we were outside and out of earshot of passersby.

His expression was more of shock and confusion than anything else. His Adam's apple bopped as he swallowed. "No. I thought they were from your boyfriend."

"Oh, really?" I said, feeling deflated. "I told you I'm not seeing anybody."

He shrugged. "People change their minds all the time. I thought you just weren't into me."

I looked at him and gave a small smile. He was so cute, but that was beside the point now. "I'm sorry. It's really not about you. But I think it's someone from our office. The type of notes they've been sending is somehow..."

"Hmmm..." Obi mused. "I wish I knew... But it wasn't me. Is that all?"

I was sad that he couldn't be and didn't seem to want to be helpful either. But I couldn't blame him. I nodded. "Thanks."

\*\*\*

I returned to my desk, wondering if I should ignore the note or meet this secret weirdo later, just to know finally who he is and what this was all about. He was really taking up too much head space for my liking, and not in a good way. It stopped being cute after the first day.

But what if this was just a trap...to get me to go on a date by teasing me with a secret? Or maybe all these were just calculated messages from a kidnapping group, to get me vulnerable for an attack? Or was I just being paranoid?

"You okay?" came Anita's calming voice.

I shook my head. "He sent a card today. It's weird... He says I should meet him at the Bar after work... What do you think?"

"What do you have to lose?" she reasoned. "If you're scared, I can come with you... I should probably do so anyway, just in case."

"You would?" I asked, hopeful.

"Of course. I want to know who this person is too," she smiled.

"Thanks..." I swallowed. There was nothing to worry about. After that, I was able to face my work.

\*\*\*

Then the strangest thing happened. Never in a million years would I have thought that he would reach out to me again. *And what the hell for?*

The notification that Demilade Adetunji wanted to send me a message popped up suddenly on my Instagram. What? What message? Was he the one behind the flowers, chocolates and love notes? My secret admirer? No, it couldn't be.

But it was so strange that he would be reaching out to me again, and now... When I am supposed to meet my secret admirer...who said he knows my 'secret' and is now ready to love me forever...in less than an hour. *Lord, what is this?!* I cried out in my soul.

*Resist the devil and he will flee from you...*

It was just the word I needed to be strong, and to do the right thing. I quickly objected to Lade sending me a message. I clicked through, and surely, he'd unblocked me.

Skimming through his page, I could see that he hadn't posted a lot since he stopped communicating with me, although he'd changed his bio message to read: "*Saved by grace through faith.*" It was sad for me to read that, as I wondered what could be going on with him. Did he actually love the Lord, or was he one of those phoney Christians? I hated to think that it was the latter and decided to pray for him right there and then.

Afterwards, I went ahead to block him. Our friendship was officially over and it would be unwise to entertain fellowship in any form. We both needed to work out our faith with fear and trembling.

# FORTY-NINE

I changed my mind after that and decided not to go to the Bar to meet anybody. I really didn't care what secret they thought they had about me. I had nothing to hide. And the truth was, I wasn't even interested, so there was no point.

And the following week, when I got no more cards nor flowers, I breathed a huge sigh of relief! Thank God they got the message, at last. Though it seemed like it had been Lade trying to get a hold of me again, it was still weird how he seemed to know what I was up to in the office. Could it be that he had a friend in my office? I sure hoped not!

Anyway, I managed to get him and the "secret admirer" out of my mind, to focus on my work, which was going very well. In early October, the pilot episode of "Fire On The Mountain" aired with a bang. It got one of the highest ratings recorded in Nigerian Television history, and I was super chuffed about it.

JV Media also got nominated under a new category in the Naija Urban Entertainment Awards for Best New TV Show for their crime series, "Jungle Justice", which launched in the second quarter of last year. Come November, we would be attending the prestigious award ceremony in Abuja to possibly take home an award. Anita is also the Production Manager for that show, so I was very thrilled for her.

We're now working on the season finale of "Fire On The Mountain", and the story is phenomenal. The debate at the meeting today was about whether to kill off one of the characters or just put him in a coma for a possible return to the show. It's been an ongoing debate actually, and got a bit heated, especially from Bayo, who created the obnoxious character, Alex, that the viewers loved to hate. I could go either way on that decision, so I opted to listen instead. In the end, Onyeka had decided not to kill off Alex, thinking his character could make a comeback in Season Three if not Season Two.

As the meeting concluded and we returned to our various offices, Obi got in step with me. "You're going to Abuja for the NUEA ceremony?"

"Is it compulsory?"

"Not at all. Script writers rarely go. But I like to. We could win! You should come. It'll be good exposure for you too."

"Ummm... I wasn't part of the production team, though..."

"That doesn't matter, because you're part of the team now... We'll be scripting Season Three in November, so get ready."

"Hmmm... Well, I don't have anything to wear..."

He giggled. "You're funny, you know? Believe me, no one is expecting you to outdo Genevieve... We are the unseen. Something smart will do."

I smiled. I was just having fun with him. I would see if my sister can watch Lara that weekend. "Okay, I'd love to go," I said, eventually. *Who knows who I might meet, hobnobbing with the elite?* I thought, with a big grin.

He beamed at me. "Cool!"

***

By the time November rolled around, I was showing. I'd started showing since late-October actually, but I could still keep it hidden with loose clothing. Up till now, no one had said anything to me about it, so I guess I was doing a good job with hiding it. But as I went through my closet looking for an outfit for the award ceremony, I knew I would have to sew one. I could hardly fit into anything nice anymore.

Money wasn't so tight these days, since my jobs paid well, and Temi sent money each month for housekeeping and care of his daughter. So, I did a search on Google for ankara dresses, and found a really nice style, which I got my tailor to sew for me. It was a gorgeous knee-length bell dress that hugged my midriff, which had since increased in size, and covered my belly so brilliantly. I especially loved how he'd dotted the middle belt and the base with crystals and coloured gems.

Anita was pleased that I was finally going out to have fun, and I was thrilled as well. It had been so long since I dressed up and made the effort to look beautiful. No, I didn't go back to the raggedy look I'd been sporting for the last few years. But I still wasn't one to slay every day, like Anita, who surprisingly had opted out of coming.

As we took our seats in the hall, I noticed a tall broad-shouldered frame that was so familiar, it made my stomach lurch. And my heart almost stopped when he turned and began to enter my row, accompanied by Onyeka, our Programme Director. *What is Temi doing here? And how does he know Onyeka? And what is that I'm feeling in my heart?*

I decided it was fear. Fear and guilt from keeping the secret of his child from him. I sank down lower into my seat, wishing the ground would open up and swallow me whole.

# FIFTY

"You don't seem too pleased to see me..." Temi whispered, lingering a little longer than I appreciated.

"Should I be?" I retorted, moving away from him.

He smiled. "You've been avoiding me..." It was a statement that sounded like a question. I hadn't been giving him a thought, that's what! Who has time to be avoiding somebody?

I drew in a deep breath. What was he playing at? "You left me, remember? Please, I'm trying to enjoy the ceremony." I brushed him off, as if he was a fly.

"You okay?" Obi, who was seated on the other side of me, asked.

I gave him a small smile, happy for the distraction, and the opportunity to use him to make Temi jealous, even though I didn't know why I thought it'd be a good idea. It was clear to anyone observant that Obi was into me. I know he hoped we'd connect tonight.

"Hey, I'm Temi. Onome's husband," Temi suddenly said, stretching out his hand to Obi, whose cheerful countenance instantly evaporated like mist on a sunny day. Temi, on the other hand, had a mischievous smile playing on his face, as he then put his arm around me.

With great annoyance, I removed it and sat up straight. "Will you stop it, Temi? I signed your bloody papers, so can you just leave me be?!"

# PERFECT LOVE

I looked at Obi apologetically, but he'd already sat upright, with a terse look on his face, as he kept his gaze focused on the stage. He was hurt, obviously because I never mentioned a husband to him. What was wrong with Temi, for God's sake? What was he even doing here?

"What are you even doing here?!" I whisper-shouted at him.

"I was invited."

I just shook my head. I could see Onyeka trying not to look interested, and it was clear to me that he was the culprit! Maybe he'd even asked Anita not to come so there'd be room for Temi. *But why?* What does he want with me again?

"Why?" I proceeded to ask.

"I want to celebrate my wife, na..." he said playfully, as if we weren't going through a divorce.

My annoyance peaked to irritation, though I didn't know why. I decided it was best to ignore him. I'll have to have a word with Onyeka later. I leaned closer to Obi, who like a repulsive magnet leaned away from me. I sighed and figured I'd better pray. I couldn't understand the emotions that were going through me. Whatever else, I still owed Temi love and respect, even if we were going through a divorce.

***

The ceremony couldn't end fast enough. The good thing was that we actually won the award for Best New TV Show, but the bad thing was that I still had to sit through an hour or so of the show sandwiched between Temi and Obi. Plus, I was staying at the same hotel with our crew, which now included Temi, instead of going home to my bed.

I headed straight out of the hall when the ceremony was over, losing out on the opportunity to network. I could feel a pair of eyes on me as I left, but I couldn't stop. The problem with being pregnant is that it also makes me super emotional, and well, my eyes were already full of tears, and I didn't know why...

I got into the room and just laid down on the bed, trying to think through what happened and process my emotions. It was beginning to look like Temi had been my "secret admirer". It would also make sense as to how he knew what I was up to at the office, because he had Onyeka as a spy. Who knows who else had been feeding him information about me? And does that mean he knew about my pregnancy already?

Maybe that was why he wanted me back. I so didn't want this to happen. I want him back, but not on these terms. And whatever happened to Mirabel and her baby? Does he really think he can have us both?! The thought was maddening.

Just then, there came a knock on the door. I was pretty sure of who it was. But I didn't know if I could talk to him. *God, I feel so mentally all over the place! What does he want?!*

As if in response to my question, his answer came, "Onome, please open the door. We need to talk."

# FIFTY-ONE

I wanted to tell him to go away, but I knew in my spirit it would be wrong. The least I could do was hear him out. But I was afraid of my reaction. I was afraid that he'd see right through me; that I never left nor gave up on us... That I'd been waiting for him all this time... That he'd see how vulnerable I am and walk all over me. That he'd tell me lies and break my heart again...

*God, give me grace*, I prayed in my spirit. *Perfect love casts out all fear*, He whispered.

"Lord, please give me the words to speak, and help me to listen with Your Spirit. I need You to take control of this whole thing. Let Your will be done and not mine," I prayed aloud, as I made to open the hotel room door, with a shaking hand.

And there he stood. My husband. Looking good, but vulnerable. Looking different.

Gone was the man with confidence, who seemed to be playing games with me. The man standing outside my room looked unsure, and desperate for salvation. And just like that, I melted.

I opened the door wider so he could come in. I still tried to control myself and my emotions, so I went to sit by the small desk in the room. The bed seemed too dangerous to linger near. However, there was nowhere else for him to sit.

"Onome, I've missed you..." he said, reaching for my hand. I let him hold me. "I was wrong to leave. I'm sorry. I was afraid..."

I looked away from him, not knowing what to say. I didn't

want to prompt him.

"Onome, you have to know that I love you so much! You were everything to me once. We were everything I ever wanted. But somehow, things fell apart and I didn't know how to keep us together. You were unhappy, and I didn't know how to make you happy. And I guess I gave up on trying…and for that I'm so sorry. I didn't realise how bad things had gotten until the day I came home and found you…"

He stopped to compose himself, as he'd gotten quite emotional. "I found you on our bed, dying… You tried to kill yourself and it made me feel so horrible. That I made you so miserable. And then I found out that it wasn't even about me… You were in love with someone else. It broke me."

I swallowed. I couldn't speak, but I felt really bad. Tears ran down my cheeks, and I wiped them with my free hand, still unable to look at him.

"I didn't think it was possible for us to survive that. I thought you didn't and never loved me, and never would. But you came back, and you tore the divorce papers I'd prepared…and begged me to come home. At first, I thought you were only trying to prove something to yourself, but through the counselling sessions, I saw your vulnerability again. And I saw how I'd hurt you and made you feel unloved. And I saw that we weren't over…we were just in a bad place and situation, but we could overcome it. It gave me hope."

I nodded and gave him a small encouraging smile. He wiped the tears from my eyes. "The night we made love again… Onome, you made me feel so many things… I felt blessed, that we could have this chance. That we could have more… More love ahead of us. And to be honest, I became afraid again. Afraid of failing you again."

I covered my mouth, as the emotions got the better of me and I sobbed.

"When Mirabel told me that she was pregnant, I felt… It felt like an affirmation, and an escape. I just couldn't believe that things could go back to normal and even be better for us, and that just confirmed it. At least, that's what I thought.

"It was like a blast to reality that I had been wishful thinking, dreaming of forever with you again.... And in a way, she seemed safer. Our love was different...Mirabel and I didn't have our history," he gestured between us. "Nor the promise or responsibility. But I was just being a fool... I was a fool, Onome. I don't want to be a fool anymore..."

"Oh... Okay," I swallowed. Now that he'd brought up the other woman and her baby, I had to ask. "So, you are just going to leave her with your baby? Or did you find out it's just a girl?!" I asked, sarcastically, and wished I could take it back. I knew it wasn't just that he wanted a boy, but that he wanted more children, and a boy would balance us out.

Temi flinched slightly but held my hand firmer. "Hmmm... About the baby..." he began.

# FIFTY-TWO

He was quiet for a while before he said, "There is no baby..."

I looked at him, and our eyes met and held for the longest time. I was trying to determine his true emotions, beyond the words he'd just said. Had he been disappointed that there was no baby? Had he been happy about that? What does that even mean?! Was she even pregnant, or did she lose the baby? And am I his fall back?

My heart raced, and it seemed he could read all those questions in my eyes. He swallowed. "She lied to me."

I swallowed too and withdrew my hand from his. *How could I trust this man?!* So, if she had been pregnant, would he have come back to me? Would he even care that I was pregnant for him?

"Onome. That's not why I'm here... I know what you're thinking...but I never went back to her."

I wasn't thinking that. But I didn't want to interrupt his flow. I folded my hands, so he couldn't hold me anymore. He rather put his hands on my thighs, and it took all my willpower not to remove them.

"I left because I knew you were upset and needed the space. I also needed the space to think, to get my head right and to be sure of what I wanted to do. I went to stay with my old friend, Onyeka...your Director. He'd just returned to Nigeria to work with your station, and we'd reconnected."

I nodded, surprised that I wasn't aware of his friendship with

Onyeka.

"I was actually the one who got him his apartment, through my agency," he added with a proud smile.

His small real estate business is still heavily reliant on referrals, but he's building it determinedly. It was often his excuse for returning home in the wee hours, because he was overseeing one project or the other. That and Church. So, as much as I am proud of him, I still hate what the hustle has done to us.

I listened as he continued to explain. "He had been in the States since high school and wasn't able to make our wedding. But he knows all about us. He's actually a fan of your writing and recommended you to join his team. Anyway... I've been staying with him and he's been a great help to me. I am also still seeing our counsellor... I realised from our first session that I have been fearful, but I know now that there is no fear in love..."

"What about Mirabel? You said she lied to you..."

He nodded. "Yes... She said it had been a scare, but she later thought that if I believed she was pregnant, it'd help me see how much I was losing or whatever... She'd been surprised that the counselling had made such a difference to me. Basically, she thought the baby would make me choose her. But the day I was supposed to accompany her for her doctor's visit, she claimed to have had a miscarriage. However, there had been something odd since about her "pregnancy" and I confronted her about my suspicions. That's when she admitted that she'd kept up the pretense with the hopes that I'd return to her."

"Hmmm..."

"I didn't, of course. That just convinced me about how wrong I'd been playing around with her. I actually broke it off with her in July, but I still needed to get my mind and heart right before reaching out to you..."

I swallowed. "So, you're my secret admirer?"

Temi gave a small smile. "Yeah... That didn't quite work out. I was trying to woo you again."

I shook my head, holding back a smile. "Why secret though?"

"I guess I still didn't know how to approach you then. I thought it would be romantic and get you all excited. But actually, I didn't want you excited about anyone but me. It was a bad idea..."

"Yeah, it was hard to get excited about someone else…" I said, with a small smile, realising the root of my irritation. He beamed at my revelation. "And then you even said you knew my "secret"..."

"Yeah," he swallowed. "Why didn't you tell me you were pregnant, Onome?" He sounded hurt.

"Can you blame me?" I retorted. Then softly, "I'm sorry I didn't. I didn't want that to be the reason you came back to me. Is it?"

He shook his head. "No! I was already working on 'Operation Get Onome Back' weeks before I found out! But it made me more determined...and happy, and sad. Sad that you didn't tell me. But I sort of figured why you hadn't."

"I would have told you eventually... It's not something I can hide forever," I said, with a little giggle.

"So, how far along are we?" Temi asked, as he reached for my hands again, looking intently into my eyes.

"About halfway. I find out the sex at my next appointment, which is next week."

"I don't want to know..."

I looked at him, and his eyes were deep, filled with love and an apology. He must have known how hurt I was; how his demands for a son made me feel inadequate. "Are you sure?"

And then Temi stands up from the bed and pulls me into his arms. "Onome, I love you. I just want to be happy with you... I am already overjoyed that you're carrying my baby...my second child. I don't care about the sex. Not anymore. I'm ready now. To love you...forever."

And like in a trance, I lift my head up to receive his kiss and it's fierce. It's overwhelming. And the tears are streaming undisturbed down my face as he is loving me. And I feel the Holy Spirit, like a force, binding us together, and making my heart whole again.

My hope did not disappoint… *Thank You*, my heart sings its song of praise.

# FIFTY-THREE

I wake up to the sound of my husband's hushed prayers, with his hand caressing my stomach and I smile. I lay my hand on his and he kisses my neck, and then my lips as I turn to him. It has been a long time since I woke up so happy.

"Good morning, Gorgeous," he says, after our lips separate.

"Good morning, love..." I mutter and swallow.

Last night had been amazing. Intoxicating. We'd made love like it was the end of the world and every second mattered. Or like forbidden lovers who had one last night to leave lasting memories. I didn't realise how much I'd missed him.

"What time is it?"

"Ten thirty. You missed breakfast. But we can order room service, when you're ready. Check out is not till noon," Temi replies.

I nod and sit up in bed. He gets out of bed to head to the bathroom, and his natural form reminds me of what we got up to last night. I sigh deeply. "Last night was quite...something."

He pops his head back into the bedroom and gives me a grin and wink. And I chuckle. I get out to find my Bible and devotional, which I take back to bed to read, as I do every morning. And before I start, I pray and thank God for life, love and family. Temi joins me in prayer, when he returns from the bathroom, and we study the Bible together.

Later that morning, as we are eating breakfast, a thought occurs to me.

"Babe... How did you know I was pregnant? I didn't tell anyone."

"It turns out five-year-olds are smarter than we give them credit for..." he replies cheekily.

"You mean... *Lara* told you?!"

He nods. "She sure did. Not in a direct way. I had to put two and two together from her description of how Mommy is doing," he laughs.

"Wow... Kids are so observant. She'll be so happy to have you home with us again."

"How is she though? I miss her terribly."

"She's fine. She missed you too," I smile and sigh. "So, Onyeka? I can't believe you've been with him all this time..."

"Please don't be upset with him... He was under pressure from his friend, and he was thinking about us."

"I'm not upset. I guess I need to thank him. For being there for my husband. And family."

"Yeah... He's really tried. He actually linked me up with a multinational company in need of a Systems Analyst."

"Oh, really?"

"Yeah... The pay is twice my previous salary, and the work's so much better. I started last month."

"I guess I owe him a big thank you, then!" I gush.

And Temi beams at me. It's so good to see him so genuinely and deeply happy. And I thank God again.

***

We're on our way to my sister's place to pick up Lara. Temi and I are sitting together at the back of our taxi, catching up on each other. I haven't thanked Onyeka yet, as he took an earlier flight out of Abuja. I don't want to do so over the phone, so I guess I'll thank him on Monday at the office.

My phone rings and it's Anita. "Hey dear! We missed you yesterday."

"Yeah... I heard the good news though!"

"Yes! We won! Congrats dear," I say, beaming.

"Yes... Thanks! But I meant the other good news..."

"What other good news?"

Anita chuckles. "Aren't you and your husband back together?!"

I turn and look at Temi. "Yes, but...who told you?"

"Onyeka."

"So, you knew? Were you in on it too?!"

"No, dear. I suspected him, because of the handwriting on the card. But he told me your husband was the one trying to toast you," she laughed. "Do you think I'd give up my seat for just anyone?!"

"Oh, wow! Thanks, dear."

"As long as you're happy, hon! Is lover boy there?" she asks.

"Yes... Hold on." I pass the phone to Temi, and watch as he smiles and chuckles into it, as if he's old friends with my new bestie. When he passes it back to me, I say, "Hmmm... All you people that can keep secret!"

And she laughs out loud. "See you later, babe."

I smile at Temi afterwards, shaking my head. He pulls me into him and kisses my head. And we snuggle the rest of the way.

When we get to my sister's place, the number of cars parked on the road make me think that they are having a small party. Temi holds my hand as we walk into the compound. The children's nanny opens the door to us and tells us that the kids are upstairs playing.

But as we walk in, I see the balloons and banners saying "Congratulations!" I turn to Temi, who doesn't look surprised, but is beaming like a mischievous kid.

"Did you know about this?!" I ask him, just as my friends and family in attendance chorus "Congratulations!!!"

"What do you mean? He was the chief party planner!" Ese says, receiving me in her arms.

"I can't take all the credit! I couldn't have done it without all of you," Temi says, as he hugs Ruke, Efe and Martin, one by one.

"I'm glad you guys have worked it all out. By the way, this counts as your Baby Shower too!" Ese says with a nudge.

And I giggle, looking at my husband and our friends and family. And I see Onyeka, Anita, Chudi and even our counsellor made it too. I greet and thank everyone, before looking at the man who prepared this delightful surprise for me.

"It's our belated six years celebration, Baby. Marriage is not beans!"

And I laugh with my whole heart. Because there's no truer saying!

***

That night, before I slept, I got the inspiration to write another poem. It was about love, *perfect* love. My mind and heart had been bound and limited by a false idea of love, but with the knowledge of the truth, I have been set free. Thank You, Jesus!

## PERFECT LOVE

All my life, I thought I wanted mad love…
I thought that was real love…
And when I had the chance to show true love,
I could not and did not, because
I thought love had to feel wild and crazy.
I didn't know that the deepest love
Was felt and forged in those quiet moments;
Those mundane things and simple acts of kindness.
But I was to learn that love is faithful.
Mad love may be exhilarating,
But it lacks wisdom and sincerity.
It burns and hurts…
It seeks its own, always.
But perfect love is selfless and fearless.
It protects and it perseveres…
It's passionate alright; enough to die for another.
Perfect love is what I was created for…
But mad love was what was advertised to me.
Now my mind is renewed…
And my heart is restored…
And my spirit is reborn…
I can give and receive perfect love,
By Him alone through whom I can do all things…

# THE EPILOGUE

*"Because of the LORD's great love we are not consumed, for his compassions never fail. They are new every morning; great is your faithfulness…"*
(Lamentations 3:22-23 - NIV).

**31/12/2018**

Dear Diary,

It's been ages since I wrote in here. So much has happened since, and I guess I've been so preoccupied these days. I'm continuing in a new book though, because I feel it's best I start on a fresh slate and capture new memories I'll be happy to read again and again.

Well, today's my birthday!!! Happy 35th birthday to me 😁!!! I can't believe another year has gone by. And what a year it has been! So many ups and downs, but at least this time around, there was massive progress too. On all fronts.

There's so much I'm thankful for. First of all, I'm thankful for life! That I'm alive today is a miracle and evidence of God's grace upon my life. I'm thankful for salvation. For knowing Jesus, who loves me in all my forms and has shown me His great mercy time and again.

I'm also thankful for Temi, my wonderful, loving and forgiving husband. This year has just made me appreciate him so much more. We started and are continuing with marriage counselling, and I've learned so much.  For one, financial intimacy was really an issue for us, because of our different backgrounds and attitudes to making and spending money.  We had so little unity, but counselling has really helped us to understand and appreciate each other more.  I've also discovered parts of him I never knew existed, and it's been amazing.  I'm so happy that we didn't give up.

I'm thankful for my beautiful darling girl, Lara.  She's such a delight.  She has really grown into her own little person.  And yes, I'm happy to be pregnant again.  I know I've been saying I'm content with just one child and don't want another, but since I knew of my expectancy, I've been so joyful!  And God has just been opening doors and making way for both of us.

I'm now six months gone and it's been a relatively peaceful pregnancy, thank God.  We still don't know the sex of the baby.  I'm surprised Temi hasn't changed his mind on that.  Right now, we are just getting ourselves ready to welcome another addition to our family.  Lara's also very excited about having a sibling.

Christmas has been such an awesome time!  We usually stay in Lagos and celebrate with my family, but this time around we decided to go to Abeokuta to enjoy it with Temi's people, most of whom live in Ogun State or return to their villa during the festive season.  It's also Lara's first journey to see her paternal grandparents, aunties, uncles and cousins, and she's having the best time!

I have to admit, I love it here too.  It's so serene and everyone pampers me, lol!  We're going back to Lagos next week, in time for Lara to resume school.

I'm still at JV Media and Magz.  "Fire On The Mountain" is still recording high ratings and the feedback has been awesome.  We also scripted the complete Season Three of "Jungle Justice" ahead of the Christmas break.  We'll begin shooting when we resume next year.  I still manage to contribute to the editorial team and maintain my weekly column with the e-magazine, but I'm thinking of reducing it to once a fortnight, or even monthly, especially with the new baby coming...and with me getting a book publishing deal and all!!!  Haaa!!!

Yes oh!!!  The MD of FairyTales Publishers reached out to me, at the start of the month, to talk about republishing my debut novel, "Is This Love?", which I self-published last December, with them. She also wants me to work on a new title for Summer 2019! 😊 So, when I say I have lots to be grateful for this year, you better believe it!

Oh, Temi's calling me to come down for my birthday dinner with the family. Later on, we'll do fireworks before the countdown into the New Year, so I thought if I don't sneak in this time to write, I may not get to it at all before my day is over. But before I go, let me just jot down this little bit of encouragement. I hope it will be a reminder to me about where I've been and where God's taking me...

## NOTE TO MYSELF

Onome, God loves you. Yes, you. The imperfect you. The weak you. And the stronger you. He loves you in all your forms. Let that truth set you free from sin and condemnation.

Onome, God is in control. Yes, He is. All the time. Even when it seems like He isn't. Even when everything is falling apart and you think things can never be right again. He is working it all out... Just keep believing.

Onome, stop worrying. If God has called you to it, He will give you the grace through it. Trust Him. Seek Him. Choose Him. And abide in Him. That's the only way you'll bear fruit.

Onome, I love you. Love me. Look after me. We've been through so much, but we are still standing. We have great dreams, so keep on pushing. Enjoy life. Learn from your mistakes and teach others. Give grace and receive grace...

Okay, I really have to go now! Til next time xoxo

## - THE END -

*"Owe no man any thing, but to love one another: for he that loveth another hath fulfilled the law"*
(Romans 13:8).

# ABOUT THE AUTHOR

Hi, my name is Ufuoma Emerhor-Ashogbon. I am a young professional, a social entrepreneur and the Founder/CEO of Fair Life Africa Foundation, a charity that supports under-privileged children. I go by the penname, Ufuomaee. I love to write and tell stories on my blog, blog.ufuomaee.org, and I also use this avenue to share about my faith in God. I am known for writing Christian romantic fiction, with lots of drama and scandal, that challenges all to think about their lifestyle and choices. I am married to Toritseju Ashogbon, a Creative Artist and a Businessman. We have a son called Jason. We live in Lagos, Nigeria.

### CONNECT WITH ME

BECOME A PATRON: www.patreon.com/ufuomaee
AUTHOR PAGE: www.amazon.com/author/ufuomaee
FOLLOW ON FACEBOOK: @ufuomaeedotcom
TWITTER: @UfuomaeeB
INSTAGRAM: @ufuomaee
WEBSITE: www.ufuomaee.org
BLOG: blog.ufuomaee.org
EMAIL: me@ufuomaee.com

Check out my full catalogue of books at
books.ufuomaee.org

Printed in Poland
by Amazon Fulfillment
Poland Sp. z o.o., Wrocław